I0598506

The Horrors of Willville

Season 1

(5 Episodes)

By

Will Savive

Del-Grande Publishing
Hackensack, New Jersey
Copyright © 2021 Will Savive/Del-Grande
Publishing

ISBN: 978-1-7374865-0-3
ASIN: B098MPKLYC

Author's Website:

https://willsavive.com/

The Horrors of Willville

Copyright © 2021 by Will Savive

To get all the latest news on horror movies & books, join:

https://www.facebook.com/dawhistlingman

ISBN-13: 978-1-7374865-0-3

BISAC: American Horror Anthology Series

Printed in the United States of America

Season 1 – Episode 1: "The Butterfly Effect"

A young man walks down the street with a duffle bag in hand. He is wearing light brown straight-fit flex Khaki pants, a light blue buttoned-down colored shirt with the sleeves rolled up just below his elbows, with a purple/black/gray Argyle V-neck sweater vest.

It's pitch-black outside, and the streets are empty. Car traffic is minimal at best. The young man walks up to a building entrance. There are two sets of doors before entering the lobby. The first set of doors are locked. The man looks around briefly before locating the bell. He presses it three times. He cannot hear a sound but anticipates that it can be heard from inside. He waits. After a minute or so, he holds the buzzer down for a second or two. A few seconds later, a heavyset, balding, older gentleman in a white lab coat approaches the second set of doors. He has a half-eaten sandwich in his right hand and a metal clipboard in the other. He shifts the clipboard to his right hand then presses the intercom button. "Can I help you?" He asks into the speaker.

"Yes, hi," the young man says politely. "I am here to start my first day of work. I'm Jefferey."

"Oh, yes, Jefferey!" The man responds joyfully. "Come right in!" He hits a different button that opens the first set of doors.

"Sorry I've come so late at night," Jefferey laments. "It's just, I was so eager to start that I couldn't sleep. So, I figured I would just come down now."

"Actually, you are not late," the man says. "You aren't supposed to start until Monday. So, really, you are early." The man chuckles, and Jefferey chuckles awkwardly in response. "I was the same way on my first day. Well, at least I think I was. It was forty years ago, so you'll have to excuse me if it's a bit hazy. I'm Doctor Robert Lambert, the resident Medical Examiner." Dr. Lambert reaches out his right hand. Jefferey reaches his right hand out and shakes the doctor's hand.

"It's an honor to meet you, Dr. Lambert. Your reputation precedes you!"

"Let's get you acquainted," says Dr. Lambert. "After all, this is your new home. And you will be here more than your actual home." They walk into the lobby area past a calendar that reads, December 2019 (Friday the thirteenth). They walk through the large double doors—nicknamed 'the forbidden double doors' because they are for morgue personnel only. The temperature drops significantly once beyond those doors.

"What do ya got in the bag there, son?"

"I brought scrubs with me."

"Okay, great! Go into the back and change. There are a few white lab coats back there as well. One of them should fit you."

****

Minutes later, Jefferey walks into the *storage chamber*. He is fully dressed in his scrubs along with a white lab coat (which both fit him perfectly). There are five naked bodies laid out on separate metal stretchers. Three of the decedents are men, and two are women. Dr. Lambert is spacing the stretchers apart as Jefferey enters. Jefferey immediately notices a wall of lockers where the dead bodies are stored, all individually numbered. He grabs a pair of plastic shoe coverings out of a box and begins to put them on, seeing as Dr. Lamber is wearing them.

A half-filled bottle of *Johnny Walker Blue Label* sits on the table near the doctor, along with a glass filled with some of its contents. Dr. Lambert grabs hold of the glass and takes a swig.

"One of my close friends gave me a few bottles as a retirement gift," he announces. "It's my favorite. Would you like a glass?"

"No, no," Jefferey says. "I'm good."

"Good, more for me!" the doctor states. "I didn't know you were coming, so I took the liberty of having a few drinks. I think I deserve it after all these years."

"Mums the word," Jefferey says, as he motions his right hand to his lips, turning a hypothetical key and simulating throwing it away—insinuating that he will not tell anyone.

"I'm not gonna bore you with the details today, kid," Dr. Lambert says casually. "You come highly recommended from Doctor Boden, and he said you were top of your class during your training and fellowship. But I do have some tricks I can show you from all these years of doing this."

"That would be great!" Jefferey states. "So, who do we have here?" he asks, referring to the bodies.

"Oh, you came on a great night. We have some doozies tonight. But we have over here [Dr. Lambert points to the heavyset, hairy man at the end] one that tops them all. This guy is allegedly the most famous serial killer of all time, *The Countdown Killer!*"

"Get outa here?" Jefferey exclaims.

"I shit you not!" Dr. Lambert says. "Well, they are not one-hundred percent sure it is him. But that's where we come in. We have been tasked to identify him from his dental records. He bit two of his numerous victims, and I personally made that determination and examined those bodies. I have the markings, and if we can match them with him, then we have our guy."

"Wow!" Jefferey said in amazement. "Why do they think that this guy is the killer, though?"

"Have you been living under a rock for the past few days, son?" Dr. Lambert asks facetiously.

"I've been so emersed in my studies and other things that I haven't been keeping up with the news," Jefferey announces.

"Well, let me tell you!" Dr. Lambert states enthusiastically. "You know the Modus Operandi of the killer, right?"

"Yeah, something about disemboweling his victims and stapling a butterfly to their tongues."

"Bingo!" Dr. Lambert says as he becomes animated with hand gestures. "Well, this guy was found with the murder weapon in his hand, a bloodied knife with the victim's blood all over it. And, he only got caught because he apparently died of a heart attack on the scene."

"Wow, so, why do they call him *The Countdown Killer*?"

"Great question!" Dr. Lambert replies. "The first victim found had the number 219 written in blood on her chest. The next victim had 218 written on his chest in blood, and so on and so forth. Instead of counting up, he counted down, all the way down to his last victim, which had the number 3 on his chest. The media figured out early on that he was counting down to 1, which would give him the highest known body count of any serial killer. The record is currently 218. But apparently, he failed because he died before he broke the record."

"He must have had this whole city in fear!" Jefferey assumes.

"City?" Dr. Lambert says facetiously. "Try the whole damn country. I'm surprised you haven't heard much about this. It's literally been the biggest topic in the country for some time now."

"Well, thank God, we got him!" Jeffery declares.

"We are going to save him for last, though," Dr. Lambert explains, "because he

The Horrors of Willville

will take the longest. So, we will process the others then work on him."

"What about the other four decedents," Jefferey asks. "Do we need to perform autopsies on them or are we just preparing them?"

"There are two suicides," Dr. Lambert explains. "We have enough physical evidence and history that we don't need to do an autopsy. One was of natural causes. But this here, we must perform an autopsy on her."

"What happened to her?" Jefferey asks curiously.

"She was murdered, and her body was found in *Verona Park*. We need to do a full examination of her body. Go grab yourself some gloves and a mask, and we will begin processing them."

****

About two hours or so had passed. Both men are in the *storage chamber*. Both of their uniforms are covered in bloodstains from the close contact of the job. Both are wearing surgical masks, goggles, hair

11

coverings, and surgical gloves. They had just finished doing the autopsy on the female. Jefferey grabs the metal handle on locker number seven and unlocks it from left to right. He slides the metal body tray into the wall. The woman's body lies on its back, headfirst into the wall. The left toe has an identification tag on it wrapped around the left big toe by a thin string. Only two bodies remain, the body of the alleged serial killer and the young woman found dead in the park. Jefferey removes his surgical gloves and washes his hands, and dries them thoroughly.

"This work is a trip," Jefferey says as he removes his goggles and face mask. "I bet you have some crazy stories over the last forty years." Dr. Lambert has just finished washing and drying his hands. He removes his face mask and goggles.

"You have no idea," Dr. Lambert asserts.

"What's the craziest story?" Jefferey asks.

"There are too many to count. But there was this one guy who died. He dressed as a clown for a living. He actually died while entertaining kids in his clown suit. He had a heart attack right there in front of the kids. The family had him buried in the clown suit that he dropped dead in."

"That's not that strange." Jefferey declares.

"Oh, no?" Dr. Lambert says. "At the wake, the whole family dressed as clowns, as well as all of their friends. They even made us (the funeral directors) dress like clowns as well! They supplied the costumes and hired a makeup person. Now, if that's not twisted, I don't know what is?" Jefferey laughs out loud.

"Woh, and I thought I was nuts!" They both share a laugh.

BUZZ!

Suddenly, there is a prolonged buzzing coming from the front door. It wasn't just a courtesy buzz; it was a rude, crude, obnoxious buzz. Both men looked at each other, a bit puzzled as to who it could be.

"It's probably the fucking press!" Dr. Lamber sneered. "They must have found out he was brought here." Dr. Lamber leaves the room and heads for the front door. He sighs as he looks outside and sees who it is. He presses the intercom.

"What is it, Maggy?" he asks in an annoyed tone.

"Is he here, doctor?"

"Is who here?"

"Oh, come on. Just let me take one picture, and I'll be out of your hair, I promise?" She proclaims.

"How the hell did you find out?" Dr. Lamber asks.

"I have my sources," Maggy says.

"Yeah, I bet you do."

"Is anyone else out there with you?" the doctor asks.

"Hell no, just me. I promise I'll only be a minute." Dr. Lamber buzzes her in. She is an attractive female with a long light-brown trench coat on with a white shirt and jeans.

"I don't want this out until Monday, you understand? Don't go pulling no bullshit on me now."

"I promise, doc. I won't breathe a word of this until Monday. I owe you big time for this!" Maggy walks into the *prep room*. Jefferey's eyes light up. Maggy takes her coat off and drapes it over a chair. Her eyes are fixated on the body.

"Woh!" Jefferey blurts out. "You're Maggy London!"

"Is that him?" She says in awe, pointing at the body.

"I'm a huge fan of yours," Jefferey stammers.

"Who the hell are you?" she says dismissively.

"He's my replacement. I'm retiring next week, remember?"

"Oh, well, excuse me for being so rude," Maggy says apologetically. She turns her attention to Jefferey.

"I love your...broadcast," Jefferey says as he stares at her cleavage.

"Hey, kid, stop drooling, will ya!" Dr. Lamber commands.

"We are gonna be seeing a lot of each other over the next few years," says Maggy as she winks at him. Jefferey lets out a smile from ear to ear. Maggy grabs her cell phone camera from her back left pocket, steadies it, and begins taking pictures of the body. She moves around the body, taking shots from different angles. In her haste, she accidentally gets Jefferey in one of the shots.

"Jefferey, move out of the way. You don't want to be in any of these shots, believe me." Dr. Lamber says.

"Oh, don't worry, handsome. I can just crop you out," Maggy says flirtatiously. "Boy, this guy was a fucking monster, for real!" Maggy asserts. "So glad this scum bag is dead!"

"You and the rest of the city," Dr. Lamber emphasizes. "Okay, would it be okay with you if we can get back to work now, doll?" Dr. Lamber says sarcastically.

"Hey, I also heard you got the girl here that was found in the park," Maggy says.

"Don't push your luck, okay, Maggy!" Dr. Lamber warns.

****

Jefferey walks Maggy to the door and lets her out.

"I'll see you around," Jefferey says.

"You sure will!" Maggy responds again in a flirtatious manner as she winks at him.

****

Jefferey walks back into the prep room. Dr. Lambert is staring at the alleged serial killer's body.

"I'm surprised that the body is in such good shape, with it being forty-eight hours since they found him," Dr. Lambert surmises.

"Yeah, that is a bit odd," says Jefferey. "He should be more stiff and rigid." Jefferey goes over to the corpse and bends his leg at the knee. "But he is flexible even."

"Oh well," Dr. Lambert says. "He is dead nonetheless. Ya know, I often wonder why the guy stapled a butterfly to his victim's tongues. I think it has something to do with hope."

"Hope?" Jefferey responds, puzzled.

"A butterfly is a symbol of hope, life, a change for the better. I'd bet he was feeling hopeless, and he felt like a loser and took it out on the world and saw the butterfly as a symbol of killing people's hope."

"No," Jefferey says firmly. "He did it as a symbol of the *butterfly effect*."

"The butterfly effect?" Dr. Lambert says, "what is that?"

"Well, in chaos theory, the butterfly effect says that in any system, there's a sensitive dependence on initial conditions, whereas small variances in these initial conditions could have profound and divergent effects on the system's outcome. For instance, if JFK's murder was to somehow be avoided, that one event could have changed the entire world. Think of how different things would be now if that one event was avoided."

"Ah, yes," Dr. Lamber pronounces emphatically. "The world would indeed be a very different place, yes. I've never heard that concept before. Very interesting. But what does that have to do with the killer?"

"Well, he felt invisible in his life. That no one cared about or loved him. He likely had no family, or at best no family that he could turn to or would listen to him. So, this was a way for him to become significant. This was a way to make himself a God, even. He believed that he was changing so many future events by his actions."

"Well said," Dr. Lamber declares. "That's a hell of a theory, son!"

"In college, I majored in forensic psychology. It's always been my favorite subject."

"Let's take a quick break. I'm going to put this [referring to the metal clipboard he is holding] in the file room, get his file [pointing to the body] and then we can start the autopsy on this monster and see if his organs are human or not." Jefferey chuckles.

"Okay, great!" Jefferey says. "I need to go to the bathroom."

****

Dr. Lambert files the completed decedents' information in the *file room* (including all of their *body identification sheets*) and grabs the complete file on the alleged serial killer. He attaches it to the metal clipboard and heads back into the *prep room*. Dr. Lambert is looking at the chart reviewing the instructions as he enters. He lifts his head, then lowers it back to the chart, but then raises it quickly in surprise. The metal stretcher that the alleged killer's body rested on moments earlier is now empty.

"What the hell?" he whimpers and gasps. He looks around the room but sees nobody. "Jefferey!" he shouts. "Jefferey!" He does not get an answer. He walks into the hallway. He passes the entrances to the *storage chamber* on his left and the *viewing room* on his right. A few steps ahead, he comes to the double doors leading to the *lobby*, which is dark. The men's room is the first door on the left after walking through the double doors coming from the back of the morgue. Dr. Lambert calls out again, "Jefferey! Are you in there?" But still, he receives no answer.

He puts his hand on the doorknob of the men's room, but before he can turn it, he hears a noise by the coatrack station up ahead. "Jefferey?" he calls out. By now, Dr. Lambert appears a bit spooked. His heart is racing, and he is breathing heavily. Suddenly, Dr. Lambert sees a figure. "What?" Dr. Lambert says with a crackle in his voice. "What are you doing? This can't be!" he shouts. He backs up and puts his hands up. "No, no!" he screams.

SLASH, SLASH!

Dr. Lambert is slashed across the face and hands with a scalpel. He is slashed again a second time a fraction of a second later. He hits the floor hard and awkwardly, causing a loud *thud* on the ground. Dr. Lambert is now at the mercy of the killer, the most heinous serial killer on earth. He is Jack the Ripper on steroids.

****

On Monday at 7:00 am, a woman, age 60, approaches the front door of the morgue. She pulls out a keychain with a large number of keys on it. The clanging sound grows louder as she reaches out and puts the key into the keyhole. She does so for the second door as well. She makes a right and goes through the walkway that reads '*reception*' up above. She sets down her purse, removes her hat, then coat, puts her glasses on her desk, and walks over to the multiple switch grid on the wall that controls the lights to *reception*, the *lounge*, the *men's* and *women's* rooms, and the *lobby*.

Almost as soon as she flips the switches, she sees something abnormal. She couldn't identify it right away, but she knew it was something unusual. She squints her eyes and looks toward the floor in the middle of the lobby through the glass window in the *reception* area. It looks like a streak of 'shit,' she thought at first; dark streaks on the floor leading to *the forbidden double doors*. Without her glasses on, everything in the distance is a blur. Yet, she had been working there for so long that only a blind person wouldn't notice this anomaly. She reaches down on her desk and grabs her glasses, and puts them on her face. The whole time she never once looked away from the lobby floor.

She walks out into the lobby and over to the streak marks. It looks like blood, but she isn't sure. It wasn't so much frightening to her as it was odd. It's a morgue, after all. However, she quickly notices that someone had dragged a bloody body a long way from that location. She begins taking shallow, quick breathes. The substance was dry and crackly, almost resembling train tracks, in that the darker spots were parallel and set a fixed distance away from one another, shoulder-length apart, with the lesser amount of blood in between. She follows the tracks to the double doors. She uses her security keycard, which is around her neck, to open the doors. Once open, she notices that the trail continues further ahead and turns into the *Storage Chamber*. She continues ahead a few yards until she comes to the Storage Chamber doors, which are closed. She uses her security keycard again to open the doors.

She enters the room and sees that the trail turns left yet again. It is dark and hard to see where it ends. She removes her glasses used for distance, turns to her right, and pushes the light switch up.

POP!

The bright lights make a popping sound as they instantly light up the room. With the stark contrast between extremely dark and extremely bright, it takes her a few seconds to adjust her eyesight. She puts her glasses back on and exhales deeply. She turns around. She sees the blood trail end at the naked body of Dr. Lambert seated on the floor, on his backside, with his back up against the wall. His clothes are in a ball near his body. His eyes are closed, and his guts are hanging out.

She quickly puts her fingertips on her forehead and her thumbs on her jawline and lets out a horrific prolonged scream!

****

Two police officers (Officer Jackson and Officer McBride) are on the scene at the morgue securing the area. Two other officers are securing the morgue just outside the front doors. Two men in dark suits enter the morgue via the front doors. Officer McBride greats them. Both men have their badges on a chain around their necks.

"I'm Agent Foster, and this is Agent Nguyen," the first agent states. "What do we got here?"

"The Black lady over there speaking to Officer Jackson is Mary Johnson," Officer

McBride declares. "She's been the secretary here for thirty years or so. She claims that she left Friday at 5:00 pm, and returned this morning at 7:00 am, and saw this trail of blood here. She followed it to the *Storage Chamber* and found Dr. Lambert naked and Gutted. And guess what? The body of the alleged *Count Down Killer* is missing, and Dr. Lambert has a butterfly stapled to his tongue and '# 1' written in blood on his chest."

"Get the fuck outa here!" Agent Nguyen proclaims. "You're saying this fucking guy came back from the dead or something?"

"Looks that way," Officer McBride responds. Officer Jackson comes walking over at that moment.

"Did she have anything else to offer?" Agent Foster asks.

"Well, she said that Dr. Lambert was set to retire in two weeks and that his replacement, *Doctor Jefferey Corey*, was supposed to start on Monday."

"Is my dick supposed to get hard over this, or are you just tickling my balls?" Agent Nguyen says sarcastically.

"Well," Officer Jackson says, "she checked the computer system and saw that the replacement appears to have started on Friday night because his login was accessed and some information was logged under his account."

"Tell her we're gonna need the camera footage from every camera source," Agent Foster commands, "then you are relieved of your duties here. This is now an FBI matter." Agents Foster and Nguyen enter the Storage Chamber to investigate Dr. Lambert's body.

"I don't understand?" Agent Nguyen clamors. "How does he put '#1' on this guy, and there is no #2? It makes no sense!"

"Maybe this new guy, Jefferey, was snatched up and taken to a different location," Agent Foster postulates. "Maybe he was killed first. Do you remember numbers 83 and 84?"

"Right, right," Agent Nguyen replies. "They were both killed in the same location, but #83 was dumped two miles down the road."

"Exactly!" Agent Foster says. "We need a full two-mile perimeter search team.

We must locate #2 before the press does! Get the local police in on this. And keep it quiet!" Agent Nguyen heads over to speak to Officer Jackson. Agent Foster's cell phone starts ringing. He pulls it from his pocket.

"Agent Foster here."

"It's Billings, sir."

"What do you want, Billings? I'm deep in the shit over here right now!"

"You're gonna wanna hear this, sir," Agent Billings warns. "They found another body in Prospect Park. It was gutted, has a butterfly on his tongue, and has a number 2 on his chest."

"Who found it?" says Agent Foster.

"It was reported to the local police. They are on scene now."

"Great!" Agent Foster responds. "Keep the damn media away from the scene until I get there! Close off the area! No one gets in without my permission!"

"You got it, sir," Billings retorts.

"Sir," Agent Nguyen says, "there's a man up front claiming to be Dr. Jefferey Corey!"

"What?" Agent Foster says, puzzled.

****

Agents Foster and Nguyen walk up to the lobby. A man is sitting in the *lounge* area with glasses and dressed in a suit and tie. His hair is dirty blonde and parted to the side. He looks nothing like the man that past Friday who stated he was Jefferey. The man stands when he sees the agents approaching.

"How can we help you?" Agent Foster asks.

"Hello," the man says. "I am doctor Jefferey Corey. Today was supposed to be my first day on the job here as the new medical examiner. What the hell is happening?" He is confused and bewildered by the police presence and the secrecy up to this point.

"Were you here this past Friday, the 13th?" Agent Nguyen asks.

"No," Jefferey states. "Why would I be here Friday? I was supposed to start today."

"Can I see some credentials?" Agent Foster commands. Jefferey has a folder with his degrees, his driver's license, and his medical license. Agent Foster walks away for a moment with Jefferey's information and makes a phone call. Agent Nguyen stays with Jefferey.

"Have you ever met Dr. Lambert before?" Agent Nguyen asks.

"No, I was scheduled to meet him today. I know of him. I'm a huge fan of him and am looking forward to his tutelage, even though it's only gonna be for two weeks."

"It's gonna be way less than that, actually," Agent Nguyen says.

"What?" Jefferey asks. "Is he here?"

"Oh, he's here," Agent Nguyen says.

"Can I speak to him?" Jefferey asks.

"That's gonna be a tough request," Agent Nguyen says sarcastically.

"Why is that? What's going on?"

"Dr. Lamber was brutally murdered here on Friday," Agent Nguyen informs him.

"What?" Jefferey laments. His eyes well up with tears. He is frozen in shock. Agent Foster hangs up the cell phone and walks back over.

"Okay, he checks out." Agent Foster hands Jefferey back his info.

"Can someone tell me what's going on?" Jefferey cries.

"Listen," Agent Foster explains, "no one knows exactly what's going on right now. But there is a murderer on the loose, and our first priority is to find him. So just sit tight here for a while, and we will explain everything to you soon. I promise. In the meantime, you are going to need to sit tight. We are going to need to keep you in custody until we figure this out."

Suddenly, one of the officers guarding the door walks inside and over to Agent Foster.

"I have a woman here who claims to have some important information for you," the officer says. Maggy comes walking over to Agent Foster.

"Hi, I am…."

"I know who you are?" Agent Foster says. "What do you want? This is closed to the press at the moment."

"I heard this man [she points to Jefferey] outside say he is Jefferey and starting today. Well, I was here on Friday night. Dr. Lambert let me take pictures of the body, and I promised him I would not publish until today. I saw the guy who was with Dr. Lambert, who claimed he was Jefferey. He is not this man. I accidentally took a picture of him."

Maggy shows Agent Foster the picture of Jefferey. He calls Agent Nguyen over furiously.

"I wanna know who this guy is, now!" Agent Foster shouts.

****

Over at Prospect Park, the police had just started to secure and cordon off the area around the body. A crime scene truck had just pulled up. Two police officers are near the victim. The body was found in the park right by the entrance. A street with high traffic runs right past it. The body is in plain view of anyone driving by. The back of the victim's body is up against the park bench a few feet from the sidewalk. The body is the overweight man in the morgue that was thought to be the serial killer. He is naked just as he is in the morgue. He was also gutted. There is a butterfly stapled to his tongue and '#2' written on his chest.

A red SUV is the last vehicle allowed to drive past the scene. Two police cars on each side are simultaneously blocking off the area. The man in the red SUV is the imposter Jefferey—the preppy man who posed as Jefferey on Friday the thirteenth. He drives slowly past the scene, staring at the body. He slows down and lowers his sunglasses to get a better look, never coming to a complete stop. He raises his glasses continues past the next roadblock that has just been set up. He scratches his right arm where he has a tattoo of a butterfly with fangs and the words *"The Butterfly Effect"* written by it. He reaches over to the passenger seat and picks up a magazine with Maggy's picture on the cover. He stares at it for a second, then puts it back down and speeds off.

The End

Season 1 – Episode 2: "The Candy Woman"

December 1936 – Closing Arguments

The courtroom is packed to max capacity. Hundreds of patrons are outside the courthouse awaiting word from inside on the last day of the trial—the closing arguments. All of the major news outlets are waiting outside as well, looking for their first soundbite. First up is the prosecutor, *Henry Turner.*

"I've never been in your position before," Mr. Turner admits as he approaches the jury. "I don't envy you. You have, in front of you, one of the toughest decisions any human will ever have to make. To decide whether or not to take away someone's freedom." Mr. Turner turns and points to *Darla May Franks.* "But while that's weighing on your head, also remember that Darla made that decision herself. Not in one moment, but over the course of a few weeks. She intentionally poisoned her husband's candy for more than two weeks. She watched him suffer, likely finding joy and a sense of accomplishment in his cries."

"Let's start from the beginning. Darla says she sat down for dinner with her family the night before her only son, Alan's, accidental death..."

****

Saturday, April 13, 1935

It was dinner time at the Franks' home. *Edward Turner* sat at the table waiting for his wife, Darla, to serve him a plate of one of his favorite meals, chicken, rice, and carrots. Being that they lived on a farm and Edward was the owner, the chicken was about as fresh as could be.

"Alan!" Darla shouts. "Dinner is ready. Come and sit at the table."

"Coming ma," the precocious ten-year-old boy responds. Darla filled a plate up with food and put it in front of Edward.

"Thank you, dear," he says. "This looks delicious."

"I made it just the way you like it," Darla says with love. Edward was enjoying his favorite drink, *The Southside Cocktail* (a gin-based drink), and he was known to drink several each night. Before Edward could dig in, Alan came running into the kitchen.

"What did I tell you?" Darla asks. "No running in the house."

"Sorry," Alan says in a whimper. Darla had a plate already prepared and waiting at the table for Alan. As Darla returned to the stove, she overheard Edward and Alan whispering. She brought her dish over to the table and sat down. The whispers stopped abruptly as she took her seat.

"What are you two going on about?" she asks curiously.

"Oh, nothing," Alan responds suspiciously.

"Lying is not your strong suit, boy," Darla replies. She turns to Edward.

"I'm gonna take the boy out on the farm with me tomorrow," Edward explains. Darla shrugs her shoulders.

"You've taken him out plenty of times

before."

"No, I mean to start working," Edward responds.

"What?" Darla sneers. "But he is only ten years old!"

"I'm not gonna be around forever," Edward declares. "The boy needs to learn the routine now. This way, he will be ready by twenty to take charge. I've lost all my workers due to the Depression and this drought may well be the end of us."

"Edward, I forbid it!" Darla orders.

"You forbid it?" Edward chuckles. "I run this house. What I say goes! My daddy had me out on the farm working at eight!"

"Your daddy wasn't a drunk!" Darla states boldly. Edward's eyes welled up with rage.

"What did you just say, woman?" he says with a scowl.

"We said we would wait until he was twelve at least," Darla deflects. Edward gets up from the table and throws the napkin that was on his lap onto the table.

"Goddamit, woman," he shouts. "Now you listen here! I work my ass off all day out there in the field. I'm short on employees, so I have to carry more of the load. I'm in pain all day and night. This is my medication!"

"But we've talked about this, Edward," she pleads. "You said you were going to slow down on the drinking. You are not you when you are drinking."

"I don't need no God damned lectures from you! I lost my appetite." Edward leaves the kitchen with a bottle of gin and heads outside. Before he exits through the front door, Darla shouts, "I swear, Edward, if anything happens to the boy due to your drinking, you'll be sorry!" Edward scoffs as he exits the house.

****

Sunday, April 14, 1935

Young Alan was having a tough go at it out there. His tiny muscles were not used to such stress and strenuous activity. Edward decided that his first year would be doing the tedious labor necessary to run the farm. It didn't require much intelligence, only work ethic and a bit of muscle. Alan was feeding the pigs and other animals. He had seen his dad do it many times before. Edward explained it to Alan, in detail that morning, what his duties would be. By afternoon he was doing it by himself.

Darla sat and watched closely for a good part of the morning. However, she had her own chores and duties to attend to. After lunch, Edward started drinking. He usually paced himself throughout the day, but because Darla was watching most of the morning, he started boozing heavily in order to catch up. But he was not accustomed to drinking that much so fast. So, he started getting a little light-headed. He didn't like to eat big lunches because it made him tired in the afternoon. This also contributed to his abnormal drunken state.

By 3:00 pm, Edward had decided that Alan had worked enough hours for his first day on the job.

"You did a great job today, son!" Edward commended him. "You did enough for today. Here is a sip of water." Alan took a big swig. "Now you know because of this drought, we need to conserve water."

"Yes, father," the boy answers, with his thirst still unquenched. The air was so dry and friable that the dirt and grit were all up in their teeth, and their mouths were dry like they'd been sucking on cotton.

"Mother will give you more water inside. But first, go fetch me my sickle and shears out there by the tractor, and you can go to your mother." Edward had finished his bottle of gin and had another one hidden away in the barn. He hurried off to fetch it as Alan walked deep into the field to retrieve the tools. Edward entered the barn and recovered the fresh bottle of gin just in time to run into Darla, who he did not know was cleaning up in there.

"Where's Alan?" she asks. She looks in his hand and sees the bottle. "And what the hell are you doing with that while our son is out there? How irresponsible can you be? I swear you care more about that gin than your own son!"

"He is right outside," Edward pleads, a bit embarrassed that he had gotten caught. "He will be here in a minute." Alan, however, got to daydreaming. He thought about one day taking over for his father. He wanted to make him proud. He knew it was hard work, but he visioned himself growing up to be as strong as his father, maybe even more robust. 'He wouldn't need alcohol to cure his ailments,' he thought.

Just then, a faint low rumbling is heard. Alan looks down and feels the ground shaking slightly.

"What's that?" Darla asks Edward. "I have no idea," he replies. "I've never heard such a sound." Both of them rushed outside to see what was happening. Darla is more concerned about where Alan is, however. They look up and see a raging black duster sweeping through the flatlands. A large dust-wave a mile high roaring toward them. Darla locates Alan, and her greatest fear has become real. Alan is in between them and the fast-approaching wave of dust and debris.

"Oh my God!" Darla screams. The wave is traveling at the speed of seventy-five MPH, and it is so thick that headlights couldn't penetrate it. Carrying large rocks and other debris, it rumbles toward the boy on its way toward the house.

"Alan!" Darla screams as she runs to

him.

"Alan!" Edward screams while waving his hands to get his attention. Alan hears them faintly. He looks up at them. The sound of the duster is now overwhelmingly loud, almost completely drowning out his parent's screams—even though they were only about fifty yards away. Alan sees his father making frantic hand gestures for him to look back and to run toward them. Alan finally turns and sees the mile-high wave of dirt and debris approaching. It is nothing like any of them had ever seen before.

Alan starts running as fast as he can toward his parents. Small step after small step he takes, but the duster gains ground quickly! Within a few seconds, it is plain to see that little Alan will not outrun this phenomenon. However, Darla is not giving up, and she is willing to sacrifice herself to get to the boy. Edward realizes that the effort is fruitless and makes a fatal decision. He tackles his wife and drags her over to the old pickup truck with no engine or wheels that Edward had serendipitously kept in that spot for years (despite Darla's constant nagging to get rid of it). Darla was always pestering him about getting rid of it.

The duster sweeps Alan up like a plastic bag in a hurricane. Edward opens the door and throws Darla into the truck. she resists the whole time. She is relentless in trying to get to Alan.

"No!" she screams. "My boy, my boy! What have you done!" Rocks and debris pelt the truck intensely. Visibility goes about as far as the window of the vehicle. Darla wails, screams, and gasps in horror. It was the longest twelve minutes of their lives.

As soon as the storm lets up, Darla races out of the truck with reckless abandonment. Edward follows close behind. She screams for her son at the top of her lungs six times, "Alan!" Soon, she came upon Alan. He was lying face down near the house. His body had been thrown and dragged nearly forty yards. He was killed almost instantly. Darla knelt there with her boy's body in her arms.

"No, Lord, please!" She screams and pleads as she rocks his little body back and forth on her knees.

****

December 1936 – Closing Arguments (resumed)

"What a horrible, horrible day that must have been!" Mr. Turner pronounces. "Could you imagine?" he shakes his head from side to side, looking somberly at the jury. "Only Darla Franks can tell you how that felt." Darla remains stone-faced. Mr. Turner begins pacing back and forth, vacillating his eyes between the onlookers and the jury.

"A mother should never have to bury her son, never, especially under such circumstances! But the unfortunate ways of life sometimes rears its ugly head. But under no circumstances, none, should premeditated murder be the answer to such a horrific event! Was Edward Franks a drunk who possibly and unintentionally caused the death of his son? Maybe. But Mr. Franks is not on trial here. Mr. Franks was murdered! He can't speak for himself. He can't give his point of view. That was taken away from him. I can give you five legitimate reasons to kill most people. That doesn't mean you do it! If Darla gets away with this, others will use this verdict as precedent. Soon, premeditated murder will become 'acceptable' as long as you have a good reason." Mr. Turner shakes his head side to side passionately.

"As sad as this case may be, you must uphold the law here today and bring back a guilty verdict," he says in a lower tone of voice than the rest of his statement. He walks right up to the jury box and speaks softly but poignantly, "It is your duty." Mr. Turner stands there for a moment, looking into the eyes of every juror and bobbing his head slightly and quickly. He then turns away and looks at the judge while walking back to his seat. "The prosecution rests, your honor."

****

December 1936 – The Verdict

The jury is seated, and the judge bangs his gavel. "Order, order." The loud crowd finally settles down to silence.

"Foreman, does the jury have a verdict," the judge asks.

"Yes, we do, your honor."

"How does the jury find the defendant?" he asks.

"We the jury find the defendant, on the count of premeditated murder, guilty," he says reluctantly. Just about everyone in the crowd jumps out of their seats and begins clamoring. The courtroom is buzzing. The judge bangs the gavel numerous times as he shouts, "order" over and over. Once he regains control of the courtroom, he lays out the sentence.

"The court has considered the defense's plea of 'insanity/grief,' and therefore, I hereby sentence Darla May Franks to thirty years in the state asylum." The crowd again erupts, and the judge bangs the gavel once more. "Court adjourned!" he says, and he quickly scurries off into his chambers, leaving mayhem behind him.

****

January 1937 – Sate Asylum

It's been a few days since Darla has been admitted to the asylum. She is isolated in her own cell. Loud sounds of mayhem fill the air. Indiscriminate chatter and sounds, such as howling and screaming, can be heard day and night. Two guards approach Darla's cell and open her door.

"Come with us!" one demands.

"Where are you taking me?" she asks timidly.

"Let's go!" the other guard orders as he grabs her arm and leads her out of the cell. They walk her downstairs and down a long hallway until they reach a room. It looks similar to a police interrogation room. The only furniture in the room are two chairs on opposite sides of a small table. They sit her down and handcuff her to the metal bar on the table. She waits there for a few moments. The room is isolated. Nothing but silence. After about ten minutes, a woman walks into the room. She is dressed in a dark blue women's suit with a skirt to match.

"Darla?" the woman asks kindly. Darla lifts her head up off of the table and looks at her with sleepy eyes. "Hi, I'm *Glenda Barnes*, the head psychiatrist at this facility." Darla remains silent. Glenda sits down and drops a large folder on the table, and crosses her legs. "Look, I know why you're here. I followed your case just like most of the people in the area. You made national news, but locally you are a future urban legend, always villainized and misunderstood. That being said, I would say that thirty to forty percent of the population understands what you did and would likely have done the same. About sixty to seventy-five percent sympathize with you, including me. We all know that the elephant in the room is the abuse that women have and continue to take from men has and will continue to go on unchecked. But that will be the forgotten part of your story. Lord knows I've been a victim myself. You think it was easy to get where I am now in this day and age?" Glenda unfolds her legs and leans forward.

"I'm here for you. You can trust me. I have to provide an evaluation of you, and I can help your stay here be a pleasant one. I would like to do that for you. Little things you need, like treats, snacks, whatever, I can do that for you. Get settled in and get some rest, and we will talk soon." Glenda gets up and walks to the door. She knocks, and the guard opens it. Darla turns and looks at Glenda. Just before she leaves the room, Darla has something to say.

"He used to get drunk and beat me at night," Darla cries out. Glenda stops in her tracks and turns around, and stares at Darla. "I know that my son, Alan, used to hear the fights," she claims. Glenda turns to the guard and gives him a head nod. She walks back in, and the guard closes the door. She sits down without saying a word. "I didn't want to do it, but I felt trapped."

"Trapped?" Glenda asks.

"With Alan gone, there was no telling how bad the abuse would have gotten. Edward started drinking even more after Alan died. It was getting worse and worse. One night, he raped me." Glenda's eyes welled up with tears. "He beat me so bad that night that I couldn't see out of my eye for almost a week. I thought I would never regain sight out of this eye," she says, pointing to her left eye.

"Look," Glenda says consolingly, "there is nothing I can say to take away your pain. But I promise you, with all my heart, that I will work with you and advocate for you. And, if the good Lord is willing, I will help you get out early from your sentence when the time is right."

"Thank you! I truly appreciate it. But I have nothing left to live for. Death for me is the best option."

"You need to hang in there, please. There are many women counting on you!"

"I will do my best if that's the case," Darla says reluctantly.

****

20-Years Later – Sate Asylum

That same room that Darla and Glenda met has changed very little. Meanwhile, everything else has changed a lot. The two women sit in the same seats they sat in twenty years before during their first meeting. They've had so many discussions and have become great friends in the last twenty years. Darla walks in casually and sits down. The difference between this entrance and her first is night and day. She looks older. She has gained a few pounds and grown a few greys. She is still very attractive, however. She looks confident and self-assured. She still has a certain reserved, elegant quality to her personality. This time, however, it comes with a much less anxious feel from onlookers. Darla sits back with her legs folded.

"I have great news!" Glenda shouts as she enters the room.

"Don't get my hopes up, please," Darla implores.

"Okay, sorry," Glenda says somberly. "I shouldn't do that; it's not fair to you. It's not that big of a deal. It's only that," she pauses for a moment, looks down, then up again, "you are getting released tomorrow!" Glenda shouts!

"You're shitting me?" Darla says in shock.

"I only shit on a toilet!" Glenda replies. "The lawyer I assigned to you got you out on good behavior. You have had a stellar record here over the past twenty years, and I wrote a nice report for you. But what really did it is the influx of new patients, causing overcrowding, they have to let some asylum veterans go, and you are one of the lucky ones." Glenda smiles.

"Oh my God," Darla shouts. "I don't know how I can ever thank you!"

"It was my pleasure," Glenda retorts. "I'm just gonna be a little sad that I won't get to see you as much. We have had some great talks over the years. I have learned much from you." Darla puts her head down and tears up. "Now, I'm sending you to my hometown. I got you a job and a place to stay. It's not much, but it will get you acclimated to the outside world. Much has changed since you first arrived here."

"A job?" Darla asks.

"Yes, you will be taking care of two young children for a working couple. I know them personally. They will provide you with housing on their premises. And the house is beautiful. They are very busy professionals and are not around much, and they are in desperate need of a nanny-slash-housekeeper."

"But what about my record? They are

okay with that?"

"No, no!" Glenda interjects. "They have no idea who you are. Your new name is Stella, and you are not to mention anything about your old life. Can you handle that?"

"Yes, yes, no mention at all. You can count on me!"

"Okay, let's get you processed and out of this shithole!" Glenda exclaims.

****

The babysitter

"Stella" (aka Darla) is sitting on the living room couch, rocking the toddler back and forth on her lap. It's her first week out of the asylum, and she is just getting used to suburban life. It doesn't hurt that the home she is living in and taking care of is luxurious. The decor is 1950s modern. The house is a four-bedroom beauty. There is an inground pool within the fenced-in backyard with all of the summer amenities one could think up.

Moreover, *Mr. and Mrs. Krane* are

very nice. They welcomed Stella with open arms. And the kids, they took a shine to her as well. They were well behaved and listened to her.

****

That night, Stella couldn't sleep. She had been having trouble adjusting to her new surroundings. She looks at the clock. It reads, 3:00 am. She gets up and walks downstairs to grab a bottle of water.

Meanwhile, two houses away from Stella, ten-year-old *Jimmy Fisher* is sleeping in his room when he hears what sounds like a small rock ricochet off of his first-floor bedroom window. He awakens but doesn't move. He isn't sure what had woken him. Seconds later, another rock bounces off of his window. And then another. He slowly creeps out of bed and approaches the window. He is afraid, but his curiosity gets the best of him.

DING!

Another rock hits as he is only a few steps from the window. He looks outside but sees nothing. He continues to look around outside when he sees three mini candy bars in mustard yellow wrapping with a red stripe around the middle sitting on his windowsill. The boy is delighted. He quickly opens the window and grabs one of the candy bars. He opens one and takes a bite. By the look on his face, it tastes great. He finishes that one then reaches out to collect the other two. Before he can reach them, the arms of a woman grab hold of the boy's arms and snatch him effortlessly out of the window. He barely makes a sound.

****

The next morning, Friday, Stella is sitting with the youngest child on the porch when two police cars come flying by and stop two houses away on the same side of the street. The mother and father of that house come running out to meet the police. The mother is first, and she is noticeably animated and upset. Stella keeps her head down and takes the toddler back inside. About an hour later, Stella goes back outside on the porch. She hears the commotion and wants to take a peek. This time, she sees a crowd of people lining the streets by the house. Police cars, and even a crime scene truck, are on hand. Yellow caution tape creates a perimeter around the home. Stella observes for a few minutes but heads back inside soon after. She is not trying to draw attention to herself.

An hour later, there is a knock at the door. Stella nervously composes herself and answers it.

"Hello, miss," the man in the police uniform says. "I'm *Sheriff Henry Parsons*. We had an incident two houses down last night. We are canvassing the block to see if anyone might have heard anything last night between the hours of 10:00 pm and 7:00 am?"

"No, sir, I did not. I was sleeping," Stella explains.

"Are Mr. and Mrs. Krane around?" he asks.

"No, they are at work."

"Who may I ask are you?" he asks politely.

"I'm the new nanny and housekeeper, sir."

"Well, congratulations," Sheriff

Parsons says. "I know most things that go on in this town. But I didn't know such a pretty lady was so close by." Stella blushes.

"Well, thank you, sir."

"Call me Henry, please," he says. "You're making me feel old with this sir stuff." Stella smiles.

"Okay, Henry."

"If you're ever in town, stop by the station and say hi," he says. "I feel more comfortable when I know the occupants of this town personally, especially the pretty ones." He winks at her.

"I will do that, Henry."

"You promise?" he asks.

"I promise," Stella says. Sheriff Parsons starts walking backwards down the stairs.

"Okay," Sheriff Parson says. "I'm holding you to that. And please pass this information along to the Krane's, and if they heard anything tell them to let me know."

"I will, and I'll see you soon," Stella says. Sheriff Parsons tips his hat and is off.

****

Later that evening, the family gathers around the table for dinner. Mrs. Krane had decided to invite Stella to dinner. The toddler sat by the misses in his highchair. Their seven-year-old son, *Conner*, and Mr. Krane are present as well. Their seven-year-old son, *Conner*, and Mr. Krane are present as well. Mrs. Krane had a splendid roast beef spread with mashed potatoes, string beans, bread, and butter on the table.

"Everything looks so great!" Stella announces.

"We haven't had an opportunity to sit down and really enjoy your presence since you arrived," Mrs. Krane says.

"I know it's only been a week," Mr. Krane states, "but we wanted to tell you how great of a job you are doing thus far."

"Yeah, the kids really like you," Mrs. Krane replies.

"Well, it's been my pleasure, really," Stella says humbly.

"Did you all hear what happened a couple houses down last night?" Mr. Krane asks.

"No," Stella replies.

"With who?" Mrs. Krane asks.

"The Fishers," Mr. Krane states. "Little Jimmy may have been abducted from his bedroom last night!"

"What?!" Mrs. Krane shouts.

"We need to be extra cautious with the kids from now on," Mr. Krane says firmly.

"Wait," Mrs. Krane commands. "What happened exactly?"

"I spoke to *Angela*. She said that the only information anyone knows is that the child's window was open all night, and he is missing."

"I need to go over there and speak to *Alice*," Mrs. Krane implores.

"I think we need to give her some time, Hun," Mr. Krane suggests. Stella keeps her head down and remains silent and disengaged. She never mentions her earlier interaction with Sheriff Parsons.

"That's just terrible," Stella interjects.

****

The following day, Stella walks down

the stairs all dressed up. It is Saturday, so Mr. and Mrs. Krane are not working. Mr. Krane is sitting on the couch reading the newspaper, and Mrs. Krane is in the kitchen. Stella's duties were limited on the weekends.

"Good morning, Stella," Mr. Krane says.

"Good morning. I am going to go into town to go shopping," Stella informs him. "I will be back in a couple of hours." Stella elegantly throws her *grey and white designer scarf* around her neck and over her left shoulder as she exits the house.

She is far away from her hometown, where she was infamous and noticeable. Even though the story of her husband's murder made national news, her release did not, and people had forgotten about her. Moreover, the way she looks changed enough in twenty years that even a person who followed the case closely back then would not recognize her today.

Stella walks into town. She purchases a few things from a few different stores. She walks into the local candy store. They have a vast array of sweets in this novelty store.

"Why, hello, Miss Stella," the old shopkeeper says politely as she walks through the door. "Nice to see you back again." Stella casually nods her head, curtsies, and tips the front of her hat. "If you're looking for those little Mary Jane candies again, we are all out," the old shopkeeper announces, speaking of the little peanut butter flavored taffy candy, with the mustard yellow wrapping with a red stripe around the middle. "Those little buggers are quite popular these days. We'll have some more tomorrow. A whole shipment, in fact."

"That's okay," Stella responds. "I still have more at home. I'm going to buy an assortment of candy today as a gift for the sheriff."

"Well, ain't that nice of ya. I can help ya pick out some of his favorites. The sheriff comes in here all the time." The old shopkeeper leans in and puts his hand by his mouth, "He's kinda got a sweet tooth," he says just above a whisper, even though there is no one else in the store. "But you didn't hear it from me."

Stella walks down the street toward the police station. She smiles and has her head held high. She has a renewed sense of purpose. She hadn't felt this special in a very, very long time. And seeing that the sheriff was fawning over her made her feel even more important. A man with such power submitting to her was intoxicating.

With the police station less than a block away, she comes to the corner of the street. Just as she does, two young children come flying around the corner on their bicycles in a tight race.

BOOM!

One of the boys collides with Stella, sending her spinning around and to the ground. The boy is ejected from his bicycle. The other boy stops for a second then races off as he sees his friend had certainly gotten himself in trouble. He wanted no part of it. Thankfully, Stella wasn't injured. The boy had only clipped her. Stella is more concerned about the candy than her own wellbeing, it seems. When she locates it, she takes a deep breath. The old shopkeeper had wrapped it very well inside its plastic housing.

"I'm sorry, I'm so sorry, ma'am!" the young boy stammers as he picks himself up off of the ground and rushes over to help her up.

"Oh, it's okay," she says. "I'm fine. Just watch where you're going from now on!" she warns. Nothing was going to get to her on that day. She brushes herself off and hurries to the police station.

****

Four children (all ten years old) walk down the sidewalk with bookbags on their backs; two boys and two girls. In this small town, most children walk to school every day. They come to a fork in the road, and after some indiscriminate chatter, one of the boys splits off from the group. He walks a bit, kicking a rock for fun until he makes a right onto a small dirt road that leads him through a small wooded area on his way home.

He is about five minutes from home. Even though the wooded area is relatively small, it is isolated. It is eerily quiet on this sunny day. Not even a bird can be heard chirping. Suddenly, a small thud. The boy stops in his tracks. He is hit in the head by a small object. He looks down. There, on the ground, lies a Mary Jane candy, still in the mustard yellow wrapping with a red stripe around the middle. He bends down and picks it up. He looks it over, then looks around. He isn't sure where it came from. He looks up and all around but sees nothing.

He takes a few more steps and notices a trail of the same candy, each about five yards apart. He picks each one of them up and continues on. He is excited by the serendipitous find. The trail leads him away from his way home, but just by a little bit. Once he has gathered several of them, one ricochets off of a tree as if it were thrown. He turns and looks in the direction that he believes it came from. He sees a slight movement in the trees up ahead. It's a blur, and he can't make out who or what it was.

"Hello?" he shouts. But no one answers. He hears the crackling of branches behind him. He turns quickly but sees nothing. He starts breathing heavily and rapidly. He changes his course quickly toward his home. He starts walking fast. Every few steps, he hears the sound of footsteps following him. Branches crackle behind him close by. He starts running in fear for his life. Seconds later, he is tackled by someone. The person turns him onto his back and straddles him. He looks up in terror. He lets out a scream, but it is brief. Silence once again rules the wooded area.

****

That night, Sheriff Parsons is sitting in his home. He is perspiring excessively and not feeling well. He pours himself a glass of bourbon and takes a swig. He is breathing heavily and struggling to take a full breath. His shirt is showing a large wet spot from shoulder to shoulder, across his chest, and up to his neck. His body is struggling to cool itself. His knees get wobbly. He struggles to stay on his feet. He grabs the table, trying desperately to hold himself up. He falls backward lifeless onto his glass coffee table, shattering it with his back on impact. The box of candy given to him by Stella is sitting on the kitchen table, open and missing several pieces of chocolate.

****

That following day, the whole town is aghast by the discoveries of the two missing bodies of the little boys. The news is all over local radio, and T.V. Word spreads fast. This town had never encountered such horrors. The barrage of bad news continues, as Sheriff Parsons' body is found in his house. The phones are ringing off the hook at the police station. *Deputy Morris* is put in charge as *interim* sheriff. Deputy Morris is sitting at his desk, looking at a picture of him and Sheriff Parsons and lamenting. A tear rolls down his cheek as his desk phone rings. He wipes it away and answers.

"Sheriff Morris, how can I help you?"

"I know who killed the two little boys and Sheriff Parsons," the woman on the line says in a low, obstinate voice.

"You what?" the sheriff asks. "Who is this?"

"Look, that woman who is staying with the Krane family; she is Darla May

Franks, the one who killed her husband by poisoning the candy."

"Who the hell is this?" the sheriff shouts.

"She was released from the asylum a couple of weeks ago, changed her name to Stella, and is there terrorizing the town. Just look into it."

"What is your name, ma..." but he gets a dial tone before he can finish his sentence. Deputy Morris immediately calls the asylum. After several minutes on hold, he finally gets to a person who can help him.

"Hello, I'm (he pauses for a second) Sheriff Morris over at the police department. I am calling to check on an inmate by the name of Darla May Franks. Is she still present at that facility?"

"Oh, no," the woman states adamantly. "She was released a couple of weeks ago due to good behavior and overcrowding."

"Okay, thanks!" Deputy Morris says in shock. He pulls the files on the three deaths and begins cross-referencing and taking notes from those cases and Stella's case. It isn't long until he finds all of the evidence he needs.

****

The following day, Stella is tending to her duties at the Krane household when she hears several very loud knocks on the door. She opens the door to find four police officers standing there with portentous looks on their faces and Mr. and Mrs. Krane with their two children.

"Darla May Franks, you're under arrest for the murders of two young boys and Sheriff Parsons!" Deputy Morris declares unwaveringly.

"What?" she asks, with a look of awe and confusion on her face.

"Are you Darla May Franks?" the sheriff asks.

"Yes, I am," she replies.

"Is this your scarf?" he asks as he raises it up to eye level.

"Yes, it is." She goes to grab it, but he moves it away.

"It was found at the crime scene in the woods."

"That's preposterous," she shouts. "I must have lost it when I was struck by a boy on his bike and fell to the ground."

"Did you not go to the candy store and buy a bag of Mary Jane candies the other day?" the sheriff asks.

"I did, so?"

"Mary Jane wrappers were found at the crime scene of the first boy's house who went missing yesterday. They were also present at the crime scene in the woods with the other boy you murdered."

"This is impossible!" Darla declares.

"Did you not buy candy for Sheriff Parsons? I was the one who escorted you in to see him."

"He was very nice to me the other day, so I decided to bring him a box of candy. Is that a crime?" she asks.

"No, it's not. Poisoning it is, however. Sheriff Parsons was found dead in his home by the box of candy you had given him. He ingested a few pieces before his death."

"Well, have it tested, and you will see it is not poisoned!" she shouts. "This is preposterous!"

"We are doing so, ma'am. In the

meantime, you must come with us!"

****

Darla awakes. She is heavily drugged up. She looks around. She is sitting back in the asylum in the same room she was told the news that she was getting out just weeks earlier. Her head bobs a bit as she is having trouble trying to keep it held upright. Her eyelids feel like they have weights on them. The door opens and closes abruptly. Darla looks up. It is Glenda.

"I'm so glad to see you," Darla says, slurring her words. Glenda sits down and crosses her legs. The look on her face is anything but empathetic.

"So, you are back again, huh?" Glenda says.

"I didn't do any of the things they accused me of, Glenda, I swear!" Darla exclaims.

"I know you didn't," Glenda states.

"So, you will help me?"

"No, Darla, I helped you already," Glenda says oddly.

"What do you mean?" Darla asks,

puzzled.

"Well, you see, you have redeemed yourself. You have paid for your crimes. You have helped eradicate a great evil from this world."

"What are you talking about?" Darla says, confused.

"You see, I'm the one who helped you get out. I'm also the reason you are back here."

"Huh?" Darla asks.

"The first time I talked to you, in this very room, I empathized with you. I knew exactly what you were going through. And I didn't think it was fair what you had been put through. But you lead with your emotions and not your head. The two are really polar opposites!"

"Can you speak English?" says Darla. "I know I'm drugged up, but I have no idea what you're talking about!"

"Sheriff Parsons was a real scumbag, let me tell you," Glenda proclaims. "You know that he raped me just after high school? He and two other men."

"What?" Darla asks.

"It's true," Glenda reveals. "You know

the two boys who were murdered?" Glenda asks. Darla just looks at her, expressionless, trying to figure out where she is going with this. "Well, the fathers of those boys joined in on the rape with the good old sheriff," Glenda discloses. Glenda is speaking in a psychotic tone. "You see, they took something from me. Something so precious that it can never be returned: my innocence. Now, Sheriff Parsons had nothing worth taking. Nothing that would have caused him the grief and pain that I've suffered over the years. So, I had to take his life."

"You did this?!" Darla shouts.

"But the other two, they had something that I could take that is tantamount to what they took from me all those years ago: their children. I've been following you these last few weeks. After you, I went into the candy store and asked the old man what you purchased and bought the same thing. I picked up your scarf after you were hit by the bicycle. I guess you forgot about it in the confusion. I poisoned the sheriffs' bourbon. He loved his bourbon so much. Nonetheless, they will attribute it to the candy you gave him. Nice touch, by the way. You paid your debt to society. You were never getting out of here anyway, Darla. You served your cosmic purpose and have redeemed yourself."

"You are sick!" Darla shouts.

"Maybe. But I'm not, and never will be, a victim. You will serve out the remainder of your sentence here, life!"

"You won't get away with this!" Darla says.

"Won't I?" Glenda replies matter-of-factly. "I never even reported the rape. You think anyone will believe you over me? A convicted murderer over a highly touted psychiatrist? And you used candy again to commit the murders. You will remain silent about this, or I will make your life so miserable in here that death will be the only thing you look forward to!" Glenda gets up and walks to the door. Darla's eyes well up with tears.

"No!" she screams!

The End

Season 1 – Episode 3: "The Curse of Lady Sonya"

There are cardboard boxes and furniture strewn all about the old house atop the steep hill. Four men from the *Lift A lot Moving Company* are racing to unload the family's belongings from their truck and call it a day. The woman in the kitchen is putting dishes and cups into the cupboards up above. She is unloading them from several boxes that read, "fragile."

The four-bedroom, three-and-a-half-bath home is the only house on the hill. A few other houses are in view from the home, but the closest one is a hundred yards away. The home has a big backyard, an inground pool, and a hot tub. A dream home for most people! Perhaps the most striking feature is the extended winding driveway that stretches almost a quarter of a mile long, in the shape of a large 'S'. About 50 yards away from the front of the house, to its northeast, is a wooded area that leads into the mountains.

There is a man outside directing the movers where to put the various items being removed from the truck. Each time he instructs one of them where to put an item, he checks the corresponding item off of his *'moving worksheet,'* which is attached to his clipboard and has been so meticulously created.

"Let me see," the man says. The mover walks over to him with a box in hand. He scans it briefly. "Second floor, first door on the left," the man directs the mover. The woman walks from the kitchen to the front yard.

"Wow, *Richard,*" the woman says. "Your little system is really working out nicely."

"I told you, Hun!" he boasts. "It's all about the symbiotic relationship between the labeling of the boxes and my clipboard here," he says, as the whipping winds shake the paper on his clipboard, seemingly on cue.

"You're such a dork," she says while giggling. "I'm gonna finish up unloading the boxes in the kitchen. I figure we will need that area free of clutter so we can have dinner in there later."

"Okay, Hun," Richard responds. He is paying more attention to the boxes and directing the movers. It's unlikely he even heard her last statement. The woman turns and walks back into the house.

"Oh, *Christina!*" Richard shouts. She peaks her head back out the doorway. "Have you called your mother to see how *Ben* is doing?"

"Yeah, a few minutes ago. She said he just ate and is taking a nap."

"Okay, great," he responds.

****

Christina takes out a roll of paper towels and some disinfectant wipes from a large round container and begins cleaning the counter and other areas. She has an ease to her movements as if she is just soaking it all in. She is content. The move was one that she wanted badly. After a few snags, Richard was able to do the things necessary to acquire the property. Christina was looking forward to this new chapter in their lives. They were in love, had a new baby, and the home of their dreams. She wanted for nothing at that moment.

As Christina cleaned the kitchen and daydreamed about how she would decorate the house, the dozen or so rocks glasses sitting upside down on the built-in kitchen island started rumbling lightly. The sound breaks Christina out of her haze. She stops what she is doing and turns her head toward the island. The low rumbling of the rim of the glasses shaking on the granite countertop is quite disorienting and unnerving. Christina freezes. Her heart begins racing. She starts taking shallow, gasping breathes. Before she can even comprehend what is happening, one of the glasses flies off of the island and onto the ground.

Smash!

Seconds later, another does the same. Then another. Christina lets out an abridged scream and leans back. The incident was over almost as soon as it began. One of the movers overhears her scream and rushes into the kitchen.

"Everything alright in here, ma'am?" he asks. Christina is still staring at the island, frozen. She shook it off seconds later.

"Um, yeah, I think so," she utters. "I just dropped a few glasses, is all."

"Oh, okay," he responds. Luckily, Christina had purchased some cleaning supplies at the dollar store on the way to the house. She grabs the broom and the dustpan. She sweeps up the broken glass off of the floor. She starts to wonder what had just happened. Surely there had to be a reasonable explanation for the incident.

****

That night, Richard peels back the covers and slides into bed wearing his matching pajamas. Seconds later, Christina walks in wearing a tight t-shirt and a thong.

"He's sleeping," she whispers.

"I know," says Richard. "I was watching you guys on the nanny cam."

"Oh, good, you set it up already!" Christina says excitedly. "First night in our new house. This is so exciting!" Christina pulls back the covers and hops into bed.

"I'm just happy that everything went well with the move," Richard says as he exhales deeply.

"Well, there was one hiccup," Christina announces.

"What happened?"

"I was in the kitchen, and the glasses started shaking."

"Shaking?" Richard asks.

"Yeah, like a dozen or so all at once. Then two of them flew off of the island in the kitchen and broke on the floor. It was very odd."

"Maybe the wind was shaking the house, and the island might be tilted. I'll check it out tomorrow. Oh, I meant to tell you!" Richard sits up quickly. "I spoke to Barry yesterday about the housekeeper. He said she is going to come by tomorrow at noon and interview with us."

"The one that used to work for his sister?" Christina asks.

"Yes, she worked for them for seven years until they bought the house in Florida, remember? They said she was great with the kids and the best housekeeper they could have ever asked for."

"Well, if Sharon said that, then it must be true," Christina says. "She doesn't ever have anything nice to say about anyone." Both of them start laughing.

"This is true," Richard says. The bathroom door in the master bedroom, which is a fraction of the way open, slowly closes all the way. The couple did not see nor hear it.

****

The next morning the couple went right to work on the house. Christina spent the morning upstairs with the baby, unpacking clothes and putting them away. Richard was busy setting up all the electronics on the first floor. He had already set up the grandfather clock. It is a beautiful showpiece. The clock struck noon. As the bell tolled, the clock immediately started playing the song, *The Westminster Quarters*, as it does every few hours. During the song, there's a knock at the door.

Clack, clack, clack.

The hammering sounded three times from someone swinging the metal doorknocker. Richard opens the door. Standing there is an incredibly beautiful young woman.

"Hi, Joanna?" Richard asks. The woman shakes her head up and down. "Come in, come in. It's so great to meet you." The woman walks in slowly and looks around anxiously. She has a small purse draped around the center of her right arm. Richard is immediately enthralled by her beauty. She is a sight to behold. She has an angelic-looking face, smooth skin, seductive eyes, a curvy body, a tiny waist, and a sexy walk. Richard also notices that she smells like vanilla and cocoa butter. The smell mesmerizes him and fires up his pleasure senses. "Christina!" Richard shouts. "Our guest has arrived. Can I get you something to drink?" he asks. She shakes her head side to side, timidly, not making eye contact.

Richard leads her into the living room.

In walks Christina seconds later.

"Hi, I'm Christina," she says as she extends her right hand. Joanna lights up when she sees Christina, and her whole demeanor changes.

"Hi, very nice to meet you!" Joanna says in a heavy Spanish accent as she shakes her hand.

"You are Joanna, right?" Christina asks.

"Yes, nice to meet you," she says again.

"Oh my God, you look so young," says Christina. "I thought you would be older." Joanna snickers.

"Please, have a seat," Richard suggests. Joanna and Christina take a seat on the couch. Richard sits on the love seat beside the couch. Joanna sits rigidly with her legs crossed.

"So, Barry tells us you worked with his sister, Sharon, for several years. She said you were a Godsend," Christina mentions.

"They are a lovely couple," Joanna states. "I grew so attached to the children. I was sad to see them go."

"Me too!" Richard laments. "Now, I will only get to see them on holidays." Joanna and Christina give off a look of sadness. "But the good news is that we get you out of the deal," Richard says.

"That's sweet," Joanna says as she flashes Richard a subtly seductive look.

"Richard and I are barely ever home at the same time," Christina explains. "We both work completely different hours. So, we need someone who can maintain the property, and especially to watch our child."

"Nothing would make me happier," Joanna declares.

"Well, you come highly recommended," says Christina. "If you want the job, it's yours."

"I would be honored," Joanna says.

"Well, let us show you around," Christina says. "Your room is on the first floor."

****

Two weeks Later

It's midnight. Richard and Christina

are getting ready for bed. Richard is in bed. Christina exits the bathroom. She pulls the covers back and gets into bed.

"Well, I think Joanna is doing a great job so far," Christina utters.

"Yeah, I think so too," Richard says. "She's just so quiet, though."

"That's a good thing," Christina suggests. "The last thing I need is a chatty Cathy or a drama queen. There is only room for one drama queen in this house."

"Ain't that the truth," Richard replies sarcastically as he rolls his eyes. Christina slaps his arm playfully, acting as if she is offended by the comment. "It just feels like she isn't here half the time. I can't explain it."

"So, let me get this straight," Christina says. "You are complaining that our housekeeper is quiet, drama-free, and barely noticeable?"

"Well, when you put it that way, it sounds strange," Richard replies.

"What is it you always tell me about referees in sports? If they go unnoticed to fans during the game, they did a great job?"

"Something like that," Richard

replies.

"Housekeeping is similar, and we are the fans. Stop whining (in Arnold Schwarzenegger's voice), as Arnold would say."

"Touché," Richard says as he shuts out the light.

****

The next day

The clock reads 6:30 pm. Richard arrived home about a half-hour before. He checked on the baby and then went downstairs to watch tv while sitting on the living room couch. He has not seen Joanna since he has been home. He did pass by her room and heard that she had her TV on. Christina works four days a week at the hospital as a nurse. This is one of the four days that she works overnight. Richard has the electronic video baby monitor with him at all times. He and Christina have the routine down very well. Joanna works from 8 am to 5 pm from Monday through Friday. Christina and Richard are happy to split the duties of taking care of their child. Joanna helps out with little Ben, but her main responsibilities center around housekeeping duties: cleaning, laundry, etc.

Richard checks on little Ben before going to bed himself. He leaves Ben's room and walks downstairs to get a drink of water before bed. He hears a strange jingle, but he cannot determine where it is coming from. It is distant. He holds still and tries to locate where the sound is coming from. 'It sounds like it's coming from the basement,' he thinks. However, just as he is getting a better idea of its location, it stops.

Not a moment later, Richard hears music playing lowly nearby. This was low but much clearer than the jingle and in a different location for sure. He knows he shouldn't snoop around, but his curiosity gets the best of him. Richard creeps down the first-floor hallway, following the music coming from the direction of Joanna's room. It's dark down the hallway just past the living room. After several light steps, Richard notices that Joanna's light is on, and her door is open about twenty-five percent of the way.

Richard walks forward slowly, trying not to be heard. As he approaches the door, he hears the music low but clearly. The piano-driven song, *'The Amorous Goldfish'* is playing from Joanna's room. It was an odd-sounding song that he had never heard before, which perplexes and intrigues him further about what was going on in that room. Observing Jonna in her natural state was an intriguing idea to him because he would get a glimpse into the character of the stranger living in his house.

Richard walks up to the door and peeks inside. Joanna has a towel wrapped around her, covering her breasts and extending down to just above her knees. Her hair is wet. With her back to Richard, she drops the towel on the floor abruptly. He gets a glimpse of her naked body. She is a perfect specimen, according to Richard's taste, and most men for that matter. She is curvy with a small waist and an apple bottom. Richard is in the dark hallway fixated on Joanna. It is as if he is frozen. Several conflicting emotions run through him at that moment. He is exhilarated, yet feels guilty. He is excited, yet feels dirty.

Joanna grabs her nightgown and slips it over her head in front of the mirror. As soon as it's on, she inadvertently looks in the mirror and notices Richard is at the door. It took Richard a few seconds to notice that she had spotted him. By the time he looks at her face in the mirror and makes eye contact with her, it is too late.

What made it a bit confusing was that she looked at him seductively. She didn't pause; she continued by sexually touching her breasts while staring at him. He immediately snaps back to reality. It was as if he was watching TV then was suddenly thrust into the scene he was watching. His head twitches briefly, and he scurries back in the direction he had come from. He felt humiliated. He immediately started thinking of what excuse he would give to his wife. He 'heard noises and simply went to check the area,' he thought. He 'had no idea that her door was open and she was naked.' Regardless, the thought of seeing her naked was so delightful that he didn't regret it at all.

Back in his bedroom, he lay in bed thinking of her, his penis fully erect. He couldn't help but touch it and think of her. Faster and faster, he stroked it as he thought about bending her over or being on top of her and hearing her moan. With great intensity, he relieved himself. The moment he was done, he felt incredibly guilty. He had been a faithful husband up until that point. He never once thought of another woman but his wife. Well, maybe a famous woman or two. Or a woman from the pornography he watched on occasion. But not from a woman he knew. And certainly not from a woman down the hall.

****

Christina worked overnight the next day as well. Richard was again home alone with the child and Joanna. He had not seen her since the awkward encounter the previous night, nor did he hear anything about it from his wife. In the back of his mind, he anticipated a call from her questioning him about the event. This caused him great anxiety throughout the workday. Having not heard anything about it, he decided he would put it out of his mind and wait to see if anything would come of it; at which point he would just play dumb.

As the night went on, Joanna never came out of her room. After watching TV for a few hours and taking care of the baby, Richard decided it was bedtime. He washed up, as he usually did. He got into bed. He again started thinking about Joanna. This time, however, he resisted the temptation to masturbate. He was tired, and he had momentarily gained some form of control, primarily due to his rising anxiety level. Before long, he was fast asleep.

He began dreaming of a woman giving him oral sex. At first, it was his wife, but then it turned into Joanna. As soon as it turned to her, he awoke briskly. He was breathing heavily, as it felt so real. He looked down, and a woman's head was under the covers between his legs bobbing up and down sensually.

"Oh honey," he said pleasurably, "you are home early."

"Mmmhm," she mouths as she continues sucking. Richard puts his head back and enjoys the experience. The sound of her wet mouth going up and down on his penis makes a series of slurping sounds.

"Damn, babe, this is something new," he announces. "Where did you learn this from, you dirty girl?" She doesn't respond. Instead, she bobs her head up and down even faster. Richard had never felt anything like it. "Oh my God, baby!" he shouts. He pulls the covers back. "I wanna see you, baby," he says passionately. She continues. Suddenly, she looks up at him. Her eyes looking right at him. "What the fuck!?" he screams.

It is Joanna!

Just as he tries to stop her, she moves her head even faster. Reason and consequences left Richard momentarily. He let go. He put his head back and let her finish. He was so close anyway. As he finishes in her mouth, he takes several deep breathes. It was the best blowjob he had ever had. Regardless, seconds later, he regains his composure. "What the fuck are you doing? Are you crazy?" he shouts.

"You seemed to like looking at me last night, so I figured I would surprise you," Joanna says.

"I'm fucking happily married," he cries. "This is totally crossing the line, Joanna!" Joanna becomes visibly upset.

"But I thought this is what you wanted!" she says. "You were thinking about me last night as you pleasured yourself!"

"I certainly was not!" Richard denies firmly. "Look, I think there has been a misunderstanding here. Why don't we forget this ever happened and just go back to normal, please?"

"How can we go back to normal after what happened?" Joanna replies. "I think we need to discuss this with your wife!" she suggests adamantly.

"No, no, no!" Richard declares, ratcheting down his tone dramatically. "Okay, maybe this was my fault," he responds.

"I think we need to tell Christina what happened," Joanna asserts.

"No!" Richard shouts. "We cannot do that. Please do not ruin my marriage. I have worked hard to get where I am!"

"You looked at me, and let me continue!" she says. "That's still cheating!

You're just like every other man, a cheating piece of shit, admit it!"

"That's entrapment!" Richard yells. "You fucking bitch! What are you trying to do?"

"Just admit you cheated, and it will all be okay," she explains.

"I swear," Richard said. He sat up and grabbed her by the throat. She was unphased. "If you say a fucking word about this, I will fucking kill you slowly and bury you in the back yard, you hear me?" Joanna shakes his right hand off of her throat easily and jumps off of the bed casually.

"Oh, yeah," she says in a creepy voice. "The only grave that's gonna be filled here is yours," she threatens with a devilish smirk on her face. Richard jumps out of bed and gives chase. Joanna rushes to the door, way ahead of him.

"Get over here, bitch!" he screams. She closes the door before he can reach it. Richard opens it immediately, but she is nowhere in sight. He runs out and stops to listen for the sounds of her footsteps. But he hears complete silence instead. She has disappeared. "You can't get away, you know!" he shouts. "We need to work this out. Cause I'm not getting a divorce over this!" Still, he hears nothing. He searches the rooms upstairs but finds nothing.

He walks downstairs, intending to check her room. Once he reaches the bottom of the stairs, he decides to check the kitchen area first, as it is closest to the stairs. However, he hears loud music coming from Joann's room. It is a piano playing the song, '*At A Georgia Camp Meeting.*' Again, the door is a quarter open, and the light is on. Richard rushes in. No one is there, however. The music (no signing) is still playing loudly, even though he could not locate a piano or a radio. He looks around. Joanna's belongings littered the room. Richard starts getting a bit dizzy; the instrumental track aided in the disorientation. He starts to feel the room spinning. The lights suddenly go out, and the door slams shut.

Bam!

Complete darkness. Fear overtakes his body. Richard gets a chill from deep inside. The strange, creepy music is still playing loudly. Richard leans up against the wall with his right hand so as to not lose his balance altogether. What seemed to him like seconds later, Richard opened his eyes. The lights are on, and the music has stopped. He is on his back, looking up at the ceiling. All of Joanna's belongings are gone. 'Did she put something in my drink?' Richard thought. The room looks completely different. He had been drinking, so he chalked it up to that and stumbled back to his bedroom.

****

The next morning Richard awoke in a haze.

"Babe, you want some coffee?" a distorted voice asks. A silhouette sat up on the side of the bed. The light shines through the window. Richard squints and raises his right hand to block the glare from his eyes. He shakes away the cob webs. Christina comes into focus. She is in her scrubs. She has just gotten home from work. Richard is still groggy. He lays his head back down for a second or two. That is until he recalls the events from the previous night.

He springs up!

"Hey, what time is it?" he asks shakily and anxiously.

"It's time for you to get up. I had a long night. You have no idea," Christina mentions. "I made you some coffee."

"Have you seen or heard from Joanna?" Richard asks.

"No, why?" she responds.

"I don't know," says Richard. "It was just weird. She told me that she got another job and that she was leaving. Before I could say goodbye, she had packed her things and left."

"Get out of here?" Christina replies, puzzled.

"I told you something was not right with her," Richard boasts.

"She left just like that?" asks Christina.

"It was so weird," Richard replies. "She said something about reaching a midlife crisis or something."

"Maybe I should call her?" Christina suggests.

"No, no!" Richard states adamantly. "She said not to come looking for her cause her decision is final. Sometimes ya just gotta let a bird spread its wings and fly away."

"What are we gonna do about a housekeeper?" Christina cautions.

"We have managed before; we will manage again until we find another one," Richard affirms. Christina walks back into the kitchen. Richard gets out of bed and gets dressed. Just as he is fully clothed, his cell phone rings. He looks at the LCD screen. It reads, 'Barry Kline.'

"Barry!" Richard exclaims. "How are ya?"

"Hey, Rit! Things are great. I'm headed to Barbados with the wife for a week. We are at the airport. She just went to the bathroom."

"That's great, good for you! Tell *Julie* I said Hello. So, things are better with you guys?"

"Ahh, something like that," Barry replies somewhat skeptically. "We are trying to work things out, and this vacation is needed by us both for sure."

"Well, that's good. I'm sure you guys will have a good time and rekindle things there."

"Hey, I wanted to check up on you and see how Joanna was working out for you all?" Barry inquires. Richard appears apprehensive about answering.

"Well, things were great, but she just up and left suddenly this morning. Said she had gotten another offer."

"She what?" Barry asks, surprised.

"Yeah, it was odd," Richard replies.

"You didn't try to make it with her, did you?" Barry asks jokingly. Richard tenses up.

"Hey, man, that's not funny!" he replies in an angry tone.

"I'm just messing with you, bud; relax." Barry chuckles. "Sorry, it didn't work out. I've tried to contact her a few times over the last couple of days, but she hasn't returned my calls." Suddenly, an announcement over the loudspeaker at the airport interrupts the call. "Okay, I gotta run," Barry says. "It's boarding time."

"Have a great vacation and good luck."

"Thanks! Keep me posted on the Joanna situation?" Barry mentions.

"Will do," Richard replies.

****

The next night Christine and Richard turned in early. At 11 pm, Christine heads upstairs. Richard begins turning off all of the lights on the first floor. When he approaches the lamp by the front window, he sees the front-yard spotlight turn on. Someone or something had tripped the outdoor spotlight sensor. When he looks closer, he sees a figure.

It is Joanna!

She is standing by the bushes staring right at Richard menacingly. More than half of the right side of her body is exposed. Only her right hand and left leg were out of view, behind the tall bush. Richard quickly turns out the light and watches. Joanna doesn't flinch. She holds her stare in his direction. Richard moves quickly to the front door. He opens it and rushes out front. "Hey!" he shouts. But he sees no one. The figure is gone. He races toward the bush, hoping to catch a glimpse of Joanna fleeing. As he reaches the spot where she was standing, he stops abruptly and looks. However, he sees no one.

For a moment, he wonders if his eyes were playing tricks on him. Yet, after a few moments of reflection, he knew for sure that the spotlight was on. And he also knew he saw someone there and that someone was almost certainly Joanna. He walks back into the house, confused. He looks back again, but no light and no Joanna. His anxiety is getting the best of him by now. He starts to believe that what happened between them was not just going to fade away benignly.

That night while sleeping, Richard tosses and turns. His mind replays the traumatizing bedroom events that occurred between him and Joanna. He keeps seeing her face look at him in the mirror as he peeks through the door. Also replaying on a loop in his head was the moment when he pulled back the covers and noticed that it was Joanna between his legs and not his wife. Richard awakens abruptly and sits up. He gasps. Christina turns toward him.

"Are you okay, Hun?" she asks. Richard is sweating and breathing heavily.

"Yeah, yeah, I'm fine," he says. "Just a bad dream. Go back to sleep." Christina closes her eyes, but Richard lies there, eyes wide open.

****

The next day, Richard decides to call Barry. It's a bright and sunny day on the beach in Barbados as Barry answers the phone.

"Hey, buddy," Barry says joyfully.

"How's it going down there?" Richard asks.

"Oh, man, the weather is amazing. We are sipping margaritas on the beach. Doesn't get any better. This trip is making the wife a little frisky also." Julie flashes Barry a sexy smile, and they lean in and kiss.

"That's great, Barry. I'll let you get back to it. I just wanted to see if you happened to get in contact with Joanna yet? I called her several times, but she is not answering. It just rings and rings and then to voicemail."

"I haven't tried," Barry says. "I will let you know if I hear anything. I will try her again now and get back to you."

"Okay, thanks," Richard says. "Go have fun." A few seconds after Richard hangs up the phone, he again hears the strange jingle that appears to be coming from the basement area. This time Richard rushes to the basement door. He swings it open, but by the time he does, the jingle has stopped. It is at this moment that Richard gets a strange feeling that there is something not right about the house. First, it was Christina's incident in the kitchen with the flying, broken glasses. The second thing that popped into his mind was all the unusual occurrences associated with Joanna's stay there. Thirdly, the strange jingle he has heard twice now. He believes it is now time to research the history of the house. It is a long shot, but he has no other options.

****

Richard pulls into the parking lot of the *Public Records* office in town. He walks inside. There are a few people lingering, and he can slip in unnoticed. He is reluctant to speak to anyone about his situation. He looks around, but unfortunately, he is a neophyte, so he decides to ask for assistance.

"Excuse me, I am looking for some information on the history of the house at *1523 Hilltop Rd.* Can you help me?"

"Sure," the male attendant replies excitedly. "There is a rich history at that house."

"You know about the house?" Richard asks.

"Of course," the attendant replies. "Everyone from here knows about that house," he says while snickering.

"What do you mean?" Richard asks.

"A woman killed her whole family in that house," he says enthusiastically. "It's a well-known urban legend. Why do you ask?"

"I live there now!" Richard replies. "I just moved in." The young attendant's eyes widen.

"Oh, wow," he says. "You need to see this!" He leads Richard to a section and pulls some microfiche data off of the shelves. "You need to go through this.

Search for articles in the late nineteenth century." The attendant writes down a few different dates. The attendant walks away and is whispering to another person and pointing at Richard. They both stare at him and appear to be gossiping.

Richard uses the wheel to scroll through several articles until he comes upon one that has his address. The article's title reads, *"Woman brutally Kills mother, husband, and son in Miss-understanding."*

****

100 Years Earlier

It was a particularly beautiful day. The warm and sultry weather brought on by the sun and relatively no clouds made for a perfect beach or pool day. Lady Sonya spent her day down at the lake, where she routinely swam and sunbathed on summer days. She once again noticed the peculiar stranger watching her bath from behind a tree. She scoffed in disgust at his insolent and adolescent behavior. On this day, however, the man approached her. Lady

Sonya rushed out of the water and quickly put on her overgarments to cover her bathing suit. The man never dared approach her before, regardless of all the times he stood watching her.

The man crept closer and closer. The closer he got to her, the more he awkwardly tried to blend in with the scenery. He acted as if he was sightseeing and not there to spy on the beautiful woman.

"Excuse me!" she shouts.

"Oh, hi, how are you? I didn't see you there," the man responds clumsily.

"You didn't see me here today, yesterday, and the other times you have been here?" she asks sarcastically. "I've seen you staring at me inappropriately many times."

"Madam, I mean no disrespect, I assure you," he says firmly. "I am actually here to bring you news. News that I regretfully have to inform you of."

"Oh really?" She says skeptically. "You've come all this way to inform me of bad news for several days but never approached me before?"

"This is because you appeared so joyful that I was reluctant to inform you those other times."

"Okay, the suspense is killing me," she says facetiously. "Please tell me."

"Your husband and your mother are having an affair," he says bluntly.

"I beg your pardon?" she replies.

"I've seen them making love in your bed several times as I regretfully went there to spy on you. I apologize that I was peeping in the window to look for you, as you are the most beautiful woman I have ever seen."

"You're telling me that you have seen this with your own eyes?" she asks. Her face turns red with anger.

"I have, Madam. It brings me no pleasure to tell you this," he laments. "I just believe that a woman with your beauty does not deserve such wretched treatment." Although, what she didn't know is that the man was lying in order to have Lady Sonya for himself, as one of his colleagues would later state he was told by the man. Lady Sonya storms off, leaving the man holding his hat! As she stormed off, his eyeballs disappeared, and his glassy eyes began glowing a shade of blue.

She walks intensely and purposefully up the S-shaped driveway that leads to her home at *1523 Hilltop Rd.* As she approaches the house, she sees her son and husband in the living room. In a rage, she grabs the gas can from the garage and begins dousing the outside of the house where the living room is located. She walks around to the front door and begins soaking the floor with gasoline on her way inside. She did so up until she passed the living room. Then, she lit a match and threw it onto the trail of gasoline.

As the fire began to blaze, Lady Sonya walks into the kitchen, grabs a large kitchen knife, and pounces her way up the stairs, completely unfazed by what she had just done. In a blind rage that she could not contain, she burst into her mother's room. Her mother is standing at the foot of the bed folding laundry onto it.

"What are you doing with that knife?" her mother asks, puzzled. Without saying a word, Lady Sonya begins stabbing her over and over again. She screams in agony as a grotesque squelching sound can be heard over and over from the knife being plunged in and out of her. During the mother's final gasps and groans, she spoke her final words, cursing her daughter to walk the earth forever, never allowed to enter heaven. From that day forward, Lady Sonya remains a lost soul. They all burned that day in the fire, including Lady Sonya. The house was rebuilt several years later.

****

After reading the article, Richard scrolls down, and his jaw drops. There, he sees a picture of the family that had died that fateful day. But to his shock and dismay, the picture of Lady Sonya is identical to the woman he knows as their housekeeper, Joanna! His heart races with fear and confusion. He jumps up and bolts out the door. He races home in his car, calling his wife's cell phone relentlessly to no avail. It went right to voicemail every time. He speeds up the S-shaped driveway, jumps out of his SUV, and runs inside.

The house is a mess. It looks like it

has been ransacked, or a struggle has ensued. Lamps are on the ground, the glass table in the living room is broken, and there is debris all over the floor.

"Christina!" he screams over and over as he searches the first floor. He runs upstairs and searches every room. "Christina!" he calls out frantically but hears only silence in return.

He runs back downstairs and decides to call Joanna's phone once again to try and clear up the situation. As he hears ringing in his cell phone receiver, so too does he hear ringing coming from the basement. By the time he reaches the basement, both ringing sounds have stopped, and he receives a standard voicemail recording. However, he notices a rotten smell coming from the basement. He heads down the stairs while he redials Joanna's phone. The ringing sounds on the phone. It also sounds nearby. He removes the phone from his ear and follows the nearby ringing sound. It leads him to a closet in the basement with French-style doors.

The ringing stops!

He looks oddly at the doors, not sure

what to think. A foul smell is very strong in that area. He opens the closet doors, and something large falls on top of him. He is so taken by surprise that he falls backward and lands on the floor. He looks up, and a dead older woman is lying on top of him. He lets out a short scream and pushes the stiff carcass off of him. He springs up and looks at the body. The basement lights flicker and then turn off. The basement becomes very dark, as no sunlight is able to penetrate the area. Richard uses his cell phone flashlight to observe the body. The woman looks as if she had been dead for a while. There is a cell phone on the floor next to her. Richard picks it up. He hits the button, and it appears to be a picture of the deceased woman with Barry's sister's kids.

Before he can process the situation, he smells smoke. He races up to the first floor and notices that there is a fire blocking the front door. He runs into the kitchen and is horrified to see his wife and baby passed out on the kitchen floor.

"What the hell!" he screams. "No, no, wake up!" he says to little Ben as he shakes him. He shakes his wife also, "Christina!"

Then he smells the strong smell of gas, which fills the room. He looks up and can see the gas thickening up the air near the oven. Panic-stricken, he picks up his wife's limp body and throws it over his left shoulder. He then grabs the baby by his shirt with his right hand and struggles to the back door of the house. The fire begins raging and spreading quickly. Smoke fills the air. Richard begins choking. He finally reaches the back door. He struggles to turn the handle as his left arm is shouldering his wife. Just as he had gotten a good grip and turns the handle, looks up through the glass on the door, and there stands Joanna, a.k.a. Lady Sonya! She has an acrimonious, evil look on her face! Her sudden appearance surprises Richard. So much so that his wife slips from his grip.

He reaches down quickly and picks her up. When he stands up straight Joanna had disappeared. Christina awakens and is groggy.

"What are you doing, Richard?" she asks.

"The house is on fire! We gotta get out of here now!" Richard shouts. Christina looks up. She is on Richard's shoulder.

"Joanna?" she says, confused.

Richard opens the door, but before he can get himself and his family outside, there is a large explosion.

BOOM!

Joanna stands nearby, watching the house collapse on itself with a menacing glare.

The End

Season 1 – Episode 4: "Escaped Murderer"

It was a busy Friday morning at the *Plumbing Supply Trust Corporation*. The payroll department was especially busy. But, by late afternoon, it had slowed significantly. Many watched the clock and conversed about their plans for the weekend, among other things. *Sally,* one of six payroll specialists (who sits in the corner cubicle), was just finishing up digitally filing the last of the electronic timesheets. Her best friend, *Sharon,* also a payroll specialist, is seated in the cubicle to her right. Sharon leans over Sally's cubicle.

"What time is *Brad* picking you up tonight?" Sharon asks.

"Shh," Sally demands as she swivels her chair to face Sharon. "Keep it down," Sally whispers. "I don't want any of these people knowing my business."

"Sorry," Sharon laments. "I'm just excited for you! Do you think he is going to propose this weekend?"

"I sure hope so," Sally responds. "It's been more than a year he's been telling me he is going to leave his wife. And now that he knows I'm pregnant with his child, I think he is really going to do it this time."

"I think so too!" Sharon says, getting all excited. "I know it's been a rough couple of years for you, and I know he wasn't happy about the baby when you broke the news to him, but I think your luck is about to turn around. I can feel it."

"I sure hope so," Sally replies. "You know I can't thank you enough for all the times you let me cry on your shoulder. You truly are my best friend. And you know you will be my Maid of Honor if he proposes."

"I better be!" Sally warns, and they both chuckle humorously. "You also need to be careful. I know you guys are headed up north, and that's where that escaped ax murderer guy is on the loose."

"I know," Sally says. "I have Brad. He is big and strong. I'd like to see that escaped killer try to mess with him. It would be a short fight. You should see how strong he is when he holds me up, and...well, you get the point."

"Woo!" Sharon shouts as she fan's herself with some papers. "You are getting me all worked up over here." They both start laughing.

Myron, the Payroll supervisor, walks over at that moment and stops in between their cubicles. He has brunette, fine hair that is parted to the side. He is wearing large-circular, somewhat stylish glasses and dressed in business attire that would hardly be considered 'well dressed.'

"Have you ladies finished all of your work for the day?" Myron asks firmly in what some would consider a moderately feminine voice.

"Myron, are we not your best employees?" Sharon asks.

"You two and Chuck, yes," Myron answers.

"So, how come you always bust our

chops and not the others?" Sharon asks sarcastically. Sally starts laughing.

"Sharon, I'm simply asking if you have finished your work. It's Friday; please don't start."

"I'm all done, Myron," Sally replies.

"Thank God I can always count on you, Sally." Myron promulgates. "You need to be more like your bestie over there, Sharon."

"You're dressed spiffy today, Myron," Sharon teases. "Do you have a big date tonight?"

"Watch it, girlfriend," Myron gests, "I'm sure H-R would love to know about this conversation."

"You wouldn't dare?" Says Sharon.

"Try me, Harlot," Myron responds as he pretends to flick his hair and walks away.

"I love that fucker!" Sharon pronounces. "But he really does need to get laid."

"Leave him alone, will ya, Sharon." Sally urges. "You are always picking on him."

"Just remember who saved him at the Christmas party last year when he was

The Horrors of Willville

drunk and caused a scene," Sharon announces to Sally just above a whisper. "It was me. He told me everything, and I counseled him. He deserves someone special. But he forgets that once he is sober and is too hung up on this job to worry about his personal life. I swear, all's he needs is one good ramming, and that stick will fall right out of his ass. You know, people are the most real when they are drunk. I know his deepest, darkest secrets, and he knows that."

"Well, remind me not to tell you what happens this weekend. You might hold that against me," Sally says as she logs out of her computer.

"You'd better tell me how it goes, or I will hunt you down, bitch." Sally smiles. "For real, though, good luck," Sharon says as she grabs her jacket from the hanger on her cubicle.

****

Brad pulls up to Sally's apartment complex in his newly leased Volvo. Sally is waiting by the curb with her suitcase in hand. Brad pops the trunk and exits the car.

"Hey, babe," he says as he kisses her on the lips and grabs her suitcase. He puts it in the trunk and gets back in the car. Within seconds they are off.

"This is so amazing," Sally says joyfully. "I'm so excited to spend the weekend with you."

"Me too, Hun," Brad responds. "I booked us a really nice hotel with a jacuzzi in the room!" Brad explains.

"I'm just happy I'm with you," Sally replies. "Where did you tell your wife where you are going?"

"I told *Erica* that I was going on a fishing trip with the boys this weekend. We don't need to talk about her."

"Okay," Sally responds. "I'm just glad I get to have this time with you."

"Me too, babe. We have a two-hour drive, so let's listen to some music."

"Okay, I'm the deejay," Sally announces. She turns on the radio and turns the station until she hears the song, *I'm Yours* by *Jason Mraz*. They both zone out as the music plays. The next song is *Just Dance*, by *Lady Gaga (featuring Colby*

O'Donis). Sally starts singing and dancing in the passenger seat. Brad looks over in amusement. Sally tries desperately to get Brad to let go and sing. It is a laborious task. However, with the next song, *Animals*, by *Maroon 5*, Sally is able to get Brad to sing along.

****

Fourteen Months Earlier

The restaurant/bar at the fancy hotel was packed that night. Adding to the plush setting was the fact that it was just two weeks until New Year's Day. The feeling of "out with the old and in with the new" was contagious. Around this time, people start thinking of the changes they are going to make in the new year.

Sally walks into the restaurant at 7:45 pm that evening.

"Hello ma'am, how can I help you?" the maître d' says politely.

"Table for two, please," Sally requests. "I'm meeting a gentleman here at 8:00 pm."

"Right this way, madam." A few moments after Sally had been seated, the skinny male waiter greets her, telling her the specials and asking her if she would like a drink.

"Sure," Sally responds. "Can I please have a rye Manhattan, up?"

"Sure thing!"

Sally sat and waited for her date. By 8:00 pm, she was getting antsy. She sends him a text message, "I'm at the restaurant seated in the corner at a small table for two. This place is very nice. Looking forward to finally meeting you!" After five minutes or so, Sally was surprised that she had not received a return text. By 8:20 pm, Sally was getting quite anxious. She decides to send him another text message, "I've been sitting here for almost a half-hour now, and I haven't even heard from you at all. At least if you're going to be late, you could have texted me and let me know." However, she still does not receive a response. By 8:45 pm (three Manhattan's later), Sally decides that she will order food. She ate dinner, settled up her tab at 9:45 pm, and headed to the bar to finish out the night. She didn't get out much, so she was in no rush to go home.

The restaurant area was thinning out by that time. However, a group of men and women, mostly men, came into the bar area. The group numbered around twenty people. They were all dressed in business apparel, and all had nametag stickers on their chests. It was at that moment that a tall, handsome, brunette gentleman caught Sally's eye. For a moment, she fantasized about having a man such as him as a husband or boyfriend. She didn't stare; she just glanced in his direction a few times. During her last glance, however, their eyes met. Sally quickly turned away no more than a second after they locked eyes.

"Would you excuse me for a second?" the man says politely to the two people he is chatting with. He walks over to the bar where Sally is sitting. "Excuse me?" he says to the bartender. "Can I have a dirty Martini, please, and whatever the lady is having?" The bartender looks at Sally.

"Me?" she asks, a bit tipsy. "No, I'm good, thanks. I've had too many already." The man signals to the bartender to pour them anyway. The bartender signals back positively by shaking his head up and down while quickly winking.

"Hi, I'm Brad."

"Hi, I'm Sally."

"Nice to meet you," Brad says. "You know, I'm pretty good at riddles, and I'm a naturally curious and inquisitive person."

"Is that so?" Sally says.

"It's true. My mother used to say that I ask way too many questions. Anyway, I'm standing over there and thought to myself, for the life of me, I can't figure out why a beautiful lady such as yourself would be sitting at a bar alone all dressed up on a Saturday night?"

"Is that a question or a statement?" she asks sarcastically as she takes the last sip of her drink. "You know what? I'll take you up on that drink." It is a timely response, as the bartender had just placed the drinks on the bar.

"I told you I'm very curious to know why," he says.

"I got stood up," the woman says somberly. "Online date. I was talking to this jerk for two weeks, and he just didn't show up."

"Wow!" Brad says as he takes a seat next to her. "What a dick!"

"Yeah, tell me about it," Sally replies. "So, what's your story? Meeting or something?"

"Business convention. Boring, but great networking opportunity." Brad reaches for his glass and takes a sip. Sally notices the ring on his finger.

"Wouldn't your wife be angry if she knew you were hitting on another woman?"

"I'm not hitting on you. I'm still aloud to talk to people of the opposite sex, no?" Both share a laugh.

"Fair enough," Sally says. "Are you happily married?"

"You know," Brad says with a gasp and a sigh, "I was once. But people grow apart. We've been having troubles lately, and we discussed splitting up. But we have been managing things for the sake of our children."

"Aww, I'm sorry to hear that," Sally says. "How long have you been married?"

"Eight years, twelve together," Brad responds. "We had some great times, and we have some great kids, but it seems as though our romance has come to an end."

The two had one drink after another, and the conversation was flowing just as fast as the alcohol. They laughed and even shed a few tears together. A genuine connection was established. Before they knew it, it was "last call" at the bar.

"Wow," says Brad, "I can't believe it's closing time already."

"Same here," Sally replies. "Where did the time go?"

"Hey, listen," Brad states in a solemn tone, "I'm not ready for this evening to end. To never see you again would bring great regret. What do you say you come up to my room, and we continue this conversation?"

"Oh, wouldn't that be appropriate?" Sally says sarcastically. "You are married, Brad. You and I could never work."

"I'm not talking about sex," he says adamantly. "I'm just talking about two lonely people who clearly have the ability to make the other forget about their problems for a short time."

"And where would we sleep, in the same bed?" Sally laughs.

"I have a suite. There are three rooms and like three different beds. There's also a jacuzzi, and I have the room booked for tonight and tomorrow night."

"Oh, big spender," Sally says, sounding drunk. Brad laughs.

"Plus, you're in no condition to get home on your own," Brad suggests.

"I'll tell you what?" Sally mentions. "I'll take you up on that offer. I think you need the help more than I do, which is pretty sad." Both share a laugh. Less than fifteen minutes later, the two would be engaged in passionate sex. Sally stayed there both nights, and the seed of love had been firmly planted.

****

On the Road Again

By now, Brad and Sally had been driving for some time. Sally had fallen asleep. Brad pulled over to get gas. He got back in the car when he was done, and Sally awoke upon him closing the door. Within seconds they were off again. Within seconds they were off again.

"Hey, sleepyhead," says Brad.

"Are we there yet?" Sally asks.

"Not yet; we have a little more than an hour to go. I just got gas."

The road that they are driving on at this point is barely two lanes. There are no street lights and no other cars on the road. Brad had shut the radio off once Sally had fallen asleep. Sally turns on the radio and turns the dial trying to find a good station. As she is doing so, a broadcast catches her attention. She stops at that station to listen.

Broadcaster: "Attention everyone in the surrounding area receiving this emergency alert. An escaped killer by the name of *Cleveland Thompson* is known to be hiding somewhere in the northern territory. Witnesses say he is wearing a white, spandex pullover mask with eye holes. If you encounter him, please do not approach him. He is armed and extremely dangerous. If you see him, please contact local authorities immediately and get somewhere safe!"

Sally lowers the radio.

"Do you believe this?" Sally asks.

"I heard he killed like thirty people, all with an ax, before they caught him," Brad mentions.

"Supposedly, he doesn't speak either, which is really creepy," Sally states. "Are we gonna be safe?" Sally asks. "Yeah, we will be fine. Don't worry. Nothing is going to happen to you while I'm around."

"Aww, you're the best baby!" Sally says, and she leans over and kisses his cheek and hugs him. "I'm so glad that you came around on the baby thing too, by the way. We are gonna have such a beautiful child! I can't wait!"

"Same here, baby," Brad says. "There is no one else in the world I'd rather have a child with. I love you so much!"

Suddenly, there is a loud popping sound resembling a gunshot, and the car starts losing speed and smoking. The vehicle comes to a halt within a few moments, and

Sally lets out a guttural scream.

"What's happening?" she asks nervously. Brad has just enough time to steer the car to the right side of the road so that half of the car is on the grass.

"I don't know," Brad says, puzzled. He tries to start the car.

Zim mim mim mim...
Zim mim mim mim...
Zim mim mim mim...

"It won't turn over," Brad says. "I think the engine blew out or something. Don't worry. I will check under the hood and see if I can fix it." Brad pops the hood and exits the car. Sally can't see what Brad is doing and is filled with anxiety. She can only see through the small inch or so crease between the raised hood and engine.

Moreover, her head is on a swivel looking around for any signs of the escaped killer. She knows it's improbable out of all of the places he could be, it was doubtful that he would stumble upon them. However, it is the area that he has been reported to have been seen last. Sally jumps as Brad slams the hood shut! He gets back in the car as Sally pulls out her phone and sees that she has no signal. She tries to make a call, but she keeps getting 'no service' after she dials and the call drops.

"Did you fix it?" she asks.

"I don't know," Brad says. He steps on the gas pedal a few times then tries to start the vehicle again.

Zim mim mim mim...

Zim mim mim mim...

"No good...shit!" Brad shouts. "Did you try your phone?"

"We get no service in this location," she explains.

"Let me try," he says. After a few seconds of trying, he says, "Mine is not working either. Okay, listen, I am going to walk back to the gas station and talk to the mechanic there. I will have him give me a ride back and see if he can fix the car. I need you to stay here."

"I'm not staying here alone! Are you fucking crazy?" Sally protests.

"It's much safer if you stay here, hun. I have no flashlight, and there are bears and coyotes out here in these woods. I can't have you pregnant and running from animals." Sally gasps, sighs, and exhales raggedly. She looks around nervously. "Look, there is a gun in the trunk if worse comes to worst. But nothing is going to happen. And if you happen to see a car, wave it down, and I'll do the same. Just keep the doors locked. I'll get you the gun." Brad pops the trunks and gets the pistol. "Have you ever used one of these?" he asks.

"Yeah, after I came back from Vietnam and the sheriff tried to run me out of town," she says. "Oh, wait, that was Rambo. No, I've never used a gun before!"

"Okay, it's easy. It is already loaded and ready to fire. All you need to do is aim and pull the trigger. But be careful not to hit the trigger until you are ready to shoot. It's very sensitive."

"I'm very sensitive right now!" Sally exclaims. "You better fucking hurry back!"

"I swear I will be back before you know it. I will try my phone along the way. If I can get a signal, I will call for help and return." Brad grabs a duffle bag from the trunk, closes it, and starts walking back toward the gas station they had just come from. Within a few seconds, Brad is out of sight.

"I'll be back before you know it," Sally says mockingly. "You're not back yet, and I know it right now!" she shouts.

****

Two Weeks Earlier

Sally is sitting on the bed at the motel getting dressed. Brad comes out of the bathroom.

"How come you never take me out on dates anymore?" Sally asks.

"Huh?" Brad asks as he looks around for his pants.

"You used to take me out every now and then, but now we just meet at the hotel and have sex. Is that all I am to you?"

"Don't start this now, Sally, please!" Brad implores.

"You never want to talk about anything," Sally complains. "Every time I bring 'us' up, you just make some face like you're annoyed and say you don't want to talk about it. You know how that makes me feel?"

"You knew what you were getting into when we started this!" Brad says adamantly.

"I did, but you said to me many times that you are going to leave her and that I am the love of your life."

"You are," Brad says. "But I have children with her. Our lives are intertwined. Do you have any idea how much money I would have to give her if we got a divorce? She hasn't worked since we had the kids. It would be a bloodbath."

"We would make it just fine," Sally says. "I work, ya know. I would be able to contribute."

"You work?" Brad says, mocking her. "You make nothing compared to what I would have to give up." Tears start coming out of Sally's eyes.

"You know, you can be such an asshole sometimes. You always have to somehow make me feel like I'm not good enough!" Sally begins balling. The tears are glistening off of her cheeks.

"Oh, I didn't mean anything by that, babe. I'm sorry." Brad sits next to her on the bed. He reaches out to her, but moves away.

"Don't touch me," she says.

"Oh, come on," he says softly. He knows what she wants is a hug, despite pulling away. She gives in almost immediately. She keeps her arms close to her chest and clenches her fists as he hugs her tightly.

"It's gonna be okay, I promise. It will all work out. Just give it some more time."

"We don't have much more time," she says softly with her head in his chest. Brad moves away.

"What do you mean?" he asks.

"Well, remember how you said that things are different because you and your wife have kids?" Brad's gaze turns very serious. He squints his eyes and tilts his head. The man who was always in control, always one step ahead, was now a helpless victim of whatever was going to come out of her mouth next. He prays it's not what he thinks it is.

"Yeah," he responds reluctantly.

"Well, I'm pregnant," Sally says as she stares at his face intently to see his response. He realizes that his prayers were not answered.

"You're what?" he blurts out.

"I'm pregnant!" she shouts.

"Are you sure it's mine?" he asks. His hands start shaking; his face is flushed of all its color.

"You're such a fucking asshole!" she screams.

"What?" he asks. "I'm just asking."

"You know I haven't been with anyone but you, dickhead!"

"What are we gonna do?" he asks.

"I'm going to have our child, Brad!"

Brad stands up and puts his right hand on his head. He walks over to the window, and Sally silently observes. He stares out of the window for a moment.

"You can't do this, Sally." He commands in an emotionless tone of voice.

"I can't do this!" she yells in anger. "I tell you I am pregnant with your child, the person you say that you love the most, and your response is 'you can't do this?' What kind of man are you?"

"This is too much for me to handle right now," he cries out.

"Too much for you to handle?" she

screams. "What about me?"

"We can just have an abortion," he suggests.

"We can?" she asks sarcastically.

"Look, I will lose everything. Erica will never let me see my kids again!" Brad shouts.

"Well, maybe she needs to know about us?" she says.

"What?" he says, bewildered.

"You heard me," she says adamantly. "Do you want to tell her, or should I?"

"I swear to God," he says with vitriol in his voice, "if you do, I will kill you!"

Sally's face is flushed of all emotion. She calmly grabs her purse, walks to the door, and opens it.

"Goodbye, Brad," she says.

"Sally, wait!" he screams. Sally slams the door. "Sally!" he yells. He runs to the door, but she is gone.

****

Back at the Car

Sally's face is flushed with fear and

anxiety. Every little noise she hears, she shutters and squints in the direction she hears it coming from. Visibility is nil. It was a cold night, and she tried desperately to keep warm. After about forty-five minutes of waiting, she was in a complete panic. Her cell phone battery is now at 10 percent. She decides that if she is going to survive this, she will need to get somewhere that has cell phone signal. She grabs her purse and readies herself for the unwanted adventure. She grips the gun handle tightly. It is the only thing that provides her any comfort.

Just as she is about to exit through the passenger side door, she notices someone standing at the driver's side door. She breathes a sigh of relief and leans over to unlock the door. The figure remains still. Her hand moves toward the unlock button, but she stops an inch before hitting it. She doesn't recognize the clothing. She thought it was Brad but notices his clothing is ragged and not compatible with Brad's outfit. Naturally, she leans in and down, trying to get a look at his face. "Brad?" she shouts. The figure stays eerily still. The figure slowly raises his right hand. What took seconds felt like hours. Within a few seconds, an ax emerges. Sally lets out a horrifying scream! "Who the fuck are you?" she shouts.

Feeling helpless, she remembers she has a gun in her hand. The figure bends down suddenly and quickly and puts his face up against the window. It is clearly a man, a big, intimidating man. He also has a white spandex mask on with two holes in it, exposing his emotionless eyes. "Back the fuck up now!" she shouts. The man stands there unphased. "I will fucking shoot you!" she warns. The man grabs the handle of the door and starts aggressively trying to open it. She looks to see if the keys are in the ignition. They are not. The figure slowly raises his left hand. What comes into her view soon after is a set of keys in the man's hand. The figure taunts her, dangling them. He puts the key in the door. Sally aims the gun at his chest and pulls the trigger.

Click!

Nothing happens. The man pauses. She pulls the trigger again, and still, no shot is fired. She pulls it again and again and again. The gun is empty. The man continues trying to unlock the door with the key. Sally screams. The driver's side door opens. The man reaches in to grab her. Sally swings the butt of the gun and hits him in his forehead. He stumbles backward. She quickly reaches for the passenger side door and is having a problem opening it.

She pushes and pulls on the handle, but it seems jammed. It isn't, though. The man shakes his head and regains his composure. He again starts moving forward. She tries her door again. This time it opens. She pushes on the door so hard that her momentum thrusts her out onto the concrete. It is a hard enough fall that it takes her a few seconds to get to her feet. By the time she does, a swinging ax is headed in her direction at close range. She barely dodges the blow. The ax hits the car door and gets stuck in it. The man pulls on it furiously, making several failed attempts to pull it free. Sally lets out a blood-curdling scream. She gets to her feet and runs straight into the woods.

She had dropped the useless gun and left her purse behind in the confusion. None of that mattered. Her only thought is to get some distance between her and her attacker. 'It is him!' she thought, the escapee. She could not believe that her luck was so bad and had led her to such a precarious situation. 'What of Brad?' she thought. 'He must be dead seeing that the man had the car keys?' She sobbed as she ran. She was not optimistic that she would survive this situation. She ran and ran but soon tired. She knew she needed to find a place to hide at some point. She looks around for the ideal spot. The woods did not present an ideal situation, however. She saw a fallen tree nearby that might provide enough cover to throw her attacker off her trail. She jumps down the small hole just under the fallen tree that provides a bit of cover.

She is breathing heavily, and her heart is racing. The hiding space was good, except it did not provide her with a possible escape route in the event that he locates her whereabouts. She peeks her eyes between the ground and the heavy log. She is looking in the direction she had come from. Suddenly, she sees the killer. He is looking around incessantly for his victim. He stops for a moment and looks in her direction. She quickly ducks her head down, trying not to be seen. She stays low for a few seconds. She takes another peek to see if he is still there.

He is gone!

She ducks her head down again. She thought that it would be a good idea to wait for a few more moments before running back to the road. Her life flashes before her eyes. She thinks about the life she could have had if this dramatic snag had not occurred. She was supposed to get a marriage proposal. This was supposed to be the happiest day of her life. Instead, she is running for her life.

She decides it is time to move. She had lost him. She slowly raises her head to take another peek. She looks out and sees the man's eyes on the other side of the tree, a foot or so away, looking right at her. She lets out a prolonged scream. She tries to scurry out of the hole, but the man is standing over her before she can. There is no escape.

"Please, please, don't kill me," she begs. "I'm with child! I'm pregnant." The man just remains motionless, staring at her.

He drops the ax and slowly removes the mask.

It is Brad!

"Brad?" she screams. "What the fuck are you doing?" Brad slowly picks up the ax after dropping the mask.

"I told you, Sally; I can't have this baby."

"What?" she says, perplexed. "So, you are going to kill me?"

"I can't go through this. I tried to tell you!" Brad laments. "I didn't want it to come to this!"

"You are fucking pathetic!" she shouts. "I can't believe you could possibly do this."

"I'm sorry, I'm sorry," he says. He extends his hand to her. "I never meant to hurt you. I was just trying to scare you." She reaches out. He pulls her out of the hole. She stands to her feet and dusts herself off.

"I can't believe this!" she states. "I can't even process this right now!" she looks up at him and sees the ax over his head. She screams! She puts her hands over her head and closes her eyes as Brad brings the ax down on her with great fury. Strike after strike, he hits her so many times that she is unrecognizable. Brad breaks down in tears as his body and face are filled with the blood of the person that he had claimed many times was the love of his life.

He walks back to the car slowly, somberly, with his head down.

"I don't know what happened?" he says to himself. "She was gone when I got back to the car. I looked everywhere for her." He is practicing his alibi. "I went back to the gas station, but it was closed!" While he was getting gas, he had asked the attendant what time they closed. He knew already; he had planned this, scouted the area, knew where there was no cell phone signal, and knew the details of the escapee's mask. While at the gas station, he rigged the car to stop. He never got gas. In fact, he ran out of gas. He knew how many miles it was until the car would run out of gas, just enough to get him to where there was no cell phone signal.

Back at the car, he went to the trunk and retrieved the gas can that he had sitting there full of gas. He filled the tank with the five-gallon gas can. He then changes his clothes and puts them back into the duffle bag. He washes off with soap, water, paper towels, and alcohol, takes the duffle bag into the woods on the opposite side, and burns and buries the contents. He walks back to the car and takes a deep breath.

A feeling of relief and calm come over him as he approaches the driver's side door. He takes a deep breath and shuffles through the keys for the front door. Suddenly he hears a strange noise. It sounds like a large piece of metal dragging across the asphalt nearby. He froze and listened. The sound continues. It is menacing and loud. He turns around. What he sees shakes him to his core. A man with an ax and a white, spandex mask with just the eyes exposed approaches. He is big and scary-looking. Even Brad, who is a big guy, is intimidated. The man in the mask has no fear of Brad. In fact, he appears to be taunting him. Brad knew that he had to make a move quickly. He races to the trunk while holding the button on the key fab to open it automatically. The trunk opens, and Brad's ax is inches away. The escapee rushes and swings his ax. Brad moves back quickly. In doing so, he falls to the ground and hits his head on the asphalt. For only a few seconds, Brad is woozy. When he regains consciousness, the last thing he sees is the ax coming down furiously on his head.

The End

Season 1 – Episode 5: "The Seven Gates of Hell"

Gate 1

On a dark night on the outskirts of town, a GS 350 SUV Lexus cruises down a dark road with no other cars in sight. The SUV is filled with youngsters in their mid-20s. The SUV pulls over slowly by a Dead-End sign that someone cleverly covered the word 'End' with yellow spray paint, leaving just the word 'Dead' showing on the sign.

They park the car and exit the vehicle. Out of the driver's seat door steps a beautiful young blonde woman. A blonde male exits via the front passenger-side door. A Black man and a Spanish man exit through each of the back seat doors. It is a lovely spring night pushing 75 degrees with no humidity. A slight breeze blows that is refreshing to all that encounter it.

"*Roger*," the woman says to the blonde gentleman. "Are you sure my car will be safe here?"

"Yeah, it will be fine, *Demi*; I told you, relax!" Roger responds.

"If all goes well, we will be in hell soon, and we won't need a car," *Clyde* jests. Everyone laughs except for Demi.

"Yeah, well, if we don't go to hell and I get a ticket, I will make sure to give you hell!" Demi says.

"I would rather go to the real hell than face your wrath!" *Jose* says.

"Roger," Clyde says, "I don't know about this, man."

"Yeah," Jose echoes, "I'm always down for some fun, wild shit, but this is a little crazy, bro."

"Stop being such pussies!" Roger retorts. "This was actually your idea, Jose!"

"It was," Jose agrees. "But I was really fucking high when I said that. How can you hold me to that?"

"You're always high!" Clyde says adamantly. Jose shrugs his shoulders in agreement.

"This is a rite of passage, people. We will be legends for doing this. As far as I know, no one has ever gone through all seven gates at nighttime and come back. Plus, do you really believe that we are going to all go to hell tonight at the same time? Take your balls out of your mom's purses."

"I'm not scared," Clyde says. He is the most muscular and strongest-looking one in the group. "God is with me. I just don't like tempting the other side, ya know?"

"I don't think God has anything to do with this place," Demi mentions.

The road they are on is dark. There are no streetlights. Each of them has a flashlight. All four walk around a slight turn and come upon a train trestle that is completely engulfed in graffiti. Trees and bushes surround it. Its tunnel is narrow, barely fitting two cars side by side at the same time. Clyde and Roger are carrying two small cooler-backpacks filled with beer.

Suddenly, a man and a woman step out of the shadows and walk over to them.

The woman is carrying a shoulder camera. The man is tall, slender, and wearing dark eyeliner. The woman has a very pale complexion, ghostly-white like. She is dressed in a gothic punk dark party dress: a retro plaid short-sleeved dress.

"Hey, are you guys here to walk the gates tonight?" he asks in a heavy English accent.

"Yeah, who are you?" Clyde asks.

"Oh, shit," Jose says, "You're *Bobby Blackhart*!"

"Yes, I am," the man answers.

"Who?" Clyde asks.

"Bobby Blackhart," Roger responds. "The famous *YouTube* guy."

"Oh shit!" Clyde shouts.

"This guy is the expert on the Seven Gates," Roger announces.

"What are you doing here?" Demi asks.

"I'm here to walk the gates. I did it during the daytime, but I haven't done it at night yet."

"Yeah," Jose says, "I saw you do it during the day on your YouTube channel. You had like four million likes!"

"I'm sure doing it at night will yield even more likes, of course. By the way, this is *Lilith*, my camera person."

"Do you mind if we walk with you and film the event?" Bobby asks.

"We would be honored!" Roger replies. Jose grabs a bunch of beers out of the cooler and passes them out.

"You will all need to sign a waiver before we begin," Bobby mentions.

"A waiver?" Demi asks.

"Yes, to allow us to film you and put it up on our channel."

"Oh damn!" Jose shouts. "We are gonna be famous!"

"This is lit for sure!" Clyde says.

"Would you guys like a beer?" Roger asks?

"No, we're good, thanks," Bobby replies. Everyone in the group signs a waiver. Soon after, Lilith throws the camera over her shoulder and begins filming.

"I will do my introduction later, and we will edit it in," Bobby tells Lilith. "Okay, guys," says Bobby, "this is the first gate."

"So, this is the first gate to hell?" Demi asks.

"Yes," Roger replies.

"Yo, this is some freaky shit!" says Jose. "Look at the fucking graffiti, man; it's cryptic." 'I (a red-shaped-heart) Satan' is spray-painted in large letters. The walls of the short tunnel are filled with graffiti of all kinds from top to bottom. There are several curse words and Satan-themed graffiti. The surrounding concrete looks like tattoos completely covering someone's arm. Just to their right lies the 'Dead' sign with the 'End' covered. However, it is meant for the street to the left of the tunnel.

"Legend has it that many years ago, a woman came driving fast toward this gate," Bobby explains. "The woman lost control of her car and slammed into the left side of the concrete wall, right here [he points to a spot on the wall]. The car caught fire, she was unable to exit the vehicle, and she burned alive."

"Oh, damn!" Clyde shouts. Jose lights up a marijuana joint and takes a few puffs. He hands it to Demi, who takes a few puffs herself.

"Trippy," she says, responding to Bobby's story, then lets out a few coughs and a cloud of smoke.

"And It is said that she guards the first gate at night," Bobby explains.

"I'm getting a very strange feeling," Jose says as he walks through the first gate, sipping on a beer.

"That's probably your hemorrhoids acting up again," Roger jests.

"No, I'm serious!" Jose says. He looks back at Roger. Behind him is a cloud of smoke taking the form of a ghastly, acrimonious-looking face. "Watch out, bro!" Jose screams. The smoke appears to be following them, Roger specifically. Roger doesn't turn around. Clyde and Demi do, however.

"Yo, what the fuck is that?" Clyde screams as he points to the cloud. Lilith turns the camera and catches the cloud of smoke that looks like an ominous face engulfing Roger from behind and then disappears. Roger, unphased, never even turns around.

"Okay, guys," Roger says, "real funny. I'm not falling for that."

"Roger!" Demi says in angst. "We are not joking around." Bobby summons Roger over to him. Lilith rewinds the tape and shows Roger.

"What is that?" Roger shouts.

"I told you, man!" Clyde shouts adamantly.

"Holy shit!" Roger says. "That thing fucking swallowed me!" Roger begins flapping his arms in front of his face as if he is furiously wiping away spider webs. His beer spills out.

"Maybe it was the kiss of death?" Bobby says and then giggles with Lilith.

"That's not funny, man!" Roger barks.

"Legend has it that the one she touches dies first tonight," Bobby says.

"That's fucking bullshit, man!" Roger screams. "Are you fucking serious?" Roger starts panicking, pacing, and walking away from the group. "I'm feeling dizzy, guys!"

"I'm just kidding ya," says Bobby. He and Lilith snicker.

"What!" Says Roger. Jose and Demi start laughing. "How is that funny?" Roger asks them.

"Dude," Clyde says to Bobby in a serious voice, "that was harsh, bro." And then he puts his right hand up to high-five

Bobby, "But funny as hell, man!"

"Oh, okay," Roger says sarcastically. "So, I'm gonna be the butt of all the jokes now?"

"Look, you guys are smoking the Devil's cigarette, and there is a bit of a drift. That's all it was. But it made for a great shot, mate."

"I don't know, man, that shit looked crazy!" Jose says.

"Looked real to me," says Demi.

Roger balls up his right fist, shakes it in front of his face, and says, "This is gonna look real to both of you in a minute when it's flying at your faces."

"Let's just keep moving. We have a long way to go," Bobby mentions.

"A long way?" Roger asks.

"Yeah, it's about an hour and forty-five-minute walk from the first gate to the seventh," Bobby explains.

"What?" Demi shouts. "I gotta walk an hour and forty-five minutes?"

"It's not that bad," says Clyde. "At least we got beer and weed."

"Yeah, but then we gotta walk back an hour and forty-five minutes as well,"

Demi states.

"Oh, shit!" Clyde says. "I didn't think of that."

"I have a friend meeting me in his SUV just past the seventh gate," Bobby says. "We will drive you back to your car."

"See," Roger says. "It's all working out fine. Now let's enjoy this. It's a once-in-a-lifetime event." Lilith chuckles. "It sure is," she says under her breath.

"Plus, if we go straight to hell getting back to the car will be the least of our worries!" Jose proclaims. Bobby points at Jose.

"Now, that's the spirit," Bobby states excitedly.

****

Gate 2

They continue walking. It was about a fifteen-minute walk to get to the second gate. Trees and forest surround them on both sides. The road is narrow, and there are no sidewalks. The road is paved, but it is years overdue from the repairs it requires.

They walk toward the second gate in groups of two. Bobby and Lilith are off getting camera shots of the surroundings. Clyde and Jose are about ten yards behind them, chatting. Behind them, about the same distance apart, Roger and Demi are walking together.

"You really got spooked back there," Demi says to Roger. "Are you alright?"

"I'm fine. It just looked weird, and I felt a little strange," Roger responds.

"You are acting different, more reserved. I know you. Something is wrong."

"My mother died in a car accident, remember?"

"Oh my God!" Demi laments. "I didn't even think of that, Hun. I'm so sorry. I wouldn't have laughed if I knew that triggered you!"

"It's not your fault," Roger replies. "I bust everyone's balls, so I'm not above a ripping. It just brought me back to that."

"Look, we don't have to go through with this," Demi informs him. "We can go back at any point."

"No, don't be silly. I love a good adventure." Clyde and Jose are up ahead, having a serious conversation.

"What do you think about that Lilith chick?" Clyde askes.

"Yeah, she's hot, man, yeah," Jose says.

"She got that tight little skirt on. Looking like a porn vampire or something," Clyde states. "I would tear that up."

"Yeah, but she is a little weird, man," Jose says.

"Weird? What you mean?"

"She hasn't said one word since they got here," Jose points out.

"What's weird about that?" Clyde says. "A hot little freak who don't talk much? Shit, where do I sign?"

"You got a point, bro," Jose agrees.

Just up ahead, Bobby and Lilith stop.

"Hey guys," Bobby screams. "Gate number two is right up here." Everyone looks up, wide-eyed, and hustles to catch up with Bibby and Lilith. As they reconvene, Gate Two is about thirty yards away, just around a slight curve in the road. Several steps later, all six are standing at the second gate.

"Here we are, ladies and gentleman,

gate number two!" Bobby pronounces. Again, graffiti lines the walls of the train trestle and is even seen on the signposts and other surrounding structures.

"What is significant about this gate," Bobby announces, "is that a woman was found here with her organs removed in the 1980s. She was allegedly part of a Satanic Ritual."

"I'm assuming she was not in attendance willingly," Roger says.

"Eww," Demi pronounces.

"No, she wasn't. Legend has it that she was dragged from her car not far from here and brought to this gate. And well, you can picture the rest," Bobby says.

"No thanks!" Jose responds.

"From what I read, the woman looked a lot like you, Demi," Bobby says in jest with a smile.

"Well, that was inappropriate," says Clyde.

"What the hell is that supposed to mean?" Demi asks, clearly offended.

"Nothing," Bobby replies. "I'm just saying that she looked a lot like you."

"How the hell do you know what she

looked like?" Demi inquires.

"I'm just saying," Bobby says. "I didn't mean to offend you."

"Just keep your personal comments to yourself from now on, okay?"

"Hey guys," Jose interrupts. "I gotta take a piss. I'll be right back." Jose runs off to the side. There is a small stream running nearby. As he is relieving himself, he feels a sharp pinch on his left leg. He flinches and looks down. He sees a large snake hissing by his left ankle. He lets out a prolonged scream and runs, pants half down, through gate number two and back to the group. He screamed the whole way through the tunnel as he managed to get his pants up and buttoned.

"I just got bit by a fucking snake, man!"

"You what?" Clyde asks.

"I was pissing, and a damn snake bit my ankle. I didn't see it well, but it was a fucking snake."

"Let me see," Demi says. She bends down and rolls up the bottom of his left jean pant leg. "Holy shit," she cries. "It's definitely a snake bite. And it's bleeding."

"What the hell?" Roger shouts. Lilith gets a good shot with the camera while Bobby is commentating about the event.

"I have some band-aids," Demi says.

"Is it poisonous?" Jose asks nervously.

"We'll know in about ten minutes," Bobby says.

"How," Clyde asks.

"Cause your man will not be able to breathe."

"It's probably not poisonous," Demi says as she bandages the bite.

"How do you know?" asks Jose.

"The number of non-lethal snakes outnumber the lethal ones by a large percentage in this area."

"Somehow, that doesn't make me feel any better," Jose says.

"Just stay calm," Roger says. "The more you panic, the faster the toxins will take effect."

"Oh, no, I'm feeling dizzy!" Jose says. He starts sweating profusely. "I'm not gonna make it!"

"Just have a seat," Demi suggests. They sit him down on an old bench nearby.

"Everything is spinning," Jose shouts.

"Breath, bro!" Clyde says. Jose's taking shallow, gasping breaths.

"Why don't you guys keep going," Clyde suggests. "I will stay here with him."

"Are you sure?" Roger asks.

"Yes," Clyde replies, "just leave me the car keys, and I'll take him to the hospital if he needs."

"Okay," Roger says. "Make sure he is okay! Call us soon and keep us updated."

Roger, Demi, Bobby, and Lilith continue on to gate number three. Morale is a bit low, but the remaining members appear to be on a mission to finish, especially now.

****

Gate 3

The remaining four participants walk the seventeen-mile trek to the next gate. Bobby and Lilith continue to gather video footage of the trip. They record the debris that has been scattered around the area. They record an abandoned couch, love seat, tires, and other junk. Empty beer cans and smoked cigarettes are everywhere.

"Where are you guys from?" Bobby askes.

"We live twenty minutes from here," Roger replies. "What about you guys?"

"We are from England," Bobby states.

"So, you guys came to *Willville* just to walk the seven gates?" Demi asks.

"Yes," Bobby responds. "If you've seen our many posts on the occult, you know that we have several popular videos on the seven gates. The gates videos are our most liked and watched videos."

"I've seen most," Roger says. "They are very informative. In fact, they are the reason most of us are here. Jose was the first to turn me on to them. Demi and I had a few drinks one night, and I showed them to her. Only Clyde came here blind."

"You guys are in for a special surprise tonight," Bobby postulates. Just before they reach gate three, Clyde and Jose come running up.

"Yo!" Clyde yells. "We are here!"

"Oh, shit, it's Jose and Clyde," Roger shouts.

"How you feeling?" Demi asks.

"No snake bite can take me out!" Jose responds. Everyone laughs.

"Are we at gate three yet, or what?" Clyde asks. Moral rises.

"Oh yes," Bobby says. "Gate three is just up ahead." Only a few steps later, the group comes upon gate number three. Again, it is graffiti-filled.

"Gate three is infamous for several hangings via the KKK," Bobby mentions. "I would have loved to be there to see these hangings."

"Excuse me?" Clyde says.

"I'm just saying that I would have loved to witness the hangings," Bobby mentions.

"So, you would have enjoyed watching Black people get hung?" Clyde asks angrily.

"I didn't mean it racially," Bobby answers.

"But it was the KKK hanging Black people," Clyde shouts. "Why do you think that would be fun to watch? Are you a fucking racist?"

"I didn't mean it like that," Bobby

replies.

"Maybe we should hang some of your family members from here and get some footage! Would you like to watch that?" Clyde emphasizes.

"All right," Roger says. "Let's take it easy."

As the group enters the narrow gate, a car comes whizzing through the tunnel. All six people quickly jump to the side. The driver could not see and did not anticipate people being inside the tunnel.

"Oh shit, heads up," Clyde screams. Roger and Demi post up against the left wall inside the tunnel, and the others do the same on the right side. The driver of the car beeps the horn as he passes.

"We must be careful of the cars that come flying through these tunnels," Bobby remarks. "Several people have died just from cars coming through."

"Thanks for telling us now, genius!" Clyde remarks sarcastically.

****

Gate 4

"Gate four is only about a three-minute walk from this gate [Gate 3]," Bobby explains to the group.

"We have been walking now for a little more than (demi looks at her watch 11:06 pm) fifty-minutes," Demi mentions. "That would mean that one or two of the next three gates is an extra-long walk."

"Or maybe four to five, five to six, and six to seven are all an equal distance walk from one another," Roger hypothesizes.

"That would mean that it will take about fifteen minutes between gates after gate four," Clyde claims.

"Actually," Bobby says, "Demi is correct. The distance between gates four and five is approximately seventeen minutes. The distance between gates six and seven is about a twenty-minute walk. Gate five to six is less than ten minutes."

"Great," Jose says. "We get longer time after gate six to think about how fucking crazy this shit is." Most in the group laugh. Within minutes the group reaches gate four.

"This is the narrowest gate of them all," Bobby mentions. "You can barely fit an SUV through this tunnel. We are gonna feel like Mexicans crossing the border in a moment."

"Hey, man!" Jose shouts. "What's your problem, dude? You have been insulting us with derogatory comments this whole time."

"I didn't mean anything by it," Bobby says with a smirk on his face. "I'm just telling you that the tunnel is small."

"Well, you got a funny way of saying things," says Jose. "And by funny, I mean not so much."

Just as they get into the tunnel, they hear a rumbling sound in the distance. The ground starts shaking. Within a few seconds, everyone yells, "Train!" The train above blows its horn. The sound of the train is distracting enough that the group does not notice the car whizzing around the bend and headed straight at them. By the time they see the lights, the car is almost on top of them. "Car!" most scream, even though the screams cannot be heard above the sound of the train.

All except for Demi post their backs tightly to the inside wall of the tunnel. Demi, however, does not see the car because she is busy readying the graffiti on the walls of the tunnel. The car is only a few feet away from her when she sees the lights. She doesn't have time to react. Clyde quickly jumps forward and pushes her back by her chest. She slams up against the wall just as the car whizzes by. Clyde's leg is still in the air and moving back toward the wall when...

Bam!

The right-side bumper collides with his left leg. Clyde lets out a prolonged scream. The two ladies in the car beep the horn incessantly after passing by. The one on the passenger side yells out of the open window, "Assholes!" Clyde falls to the ground. He is in pain.

"Oh my God, Clyde, I'm so sorry!" Demi cries.

"It's not your fault," Clyde says while grimacing and groaning.

"Is it broken, buddy?" says Jose.

"I don't know," Clyde responds.

"Let me take a look at it?" Demi says.

"It doesn't look broken," she says. "Try walking on it."

Roger and Jose help Clyde to his feet. He is limping severely.

"It's definitely not broken," Bobby says, "or you wouldn't be able to walk on it."

"Let's just keep moving," Clyde proposes.

"Are you sure?" Demi asks.

"Yeah, I'll be fine!" Clyde says.

"You saved me, Clyde," Demi declares with admiration. "Thank you so much!"

"Don't mention it," says Clyde, as he limps forward, trying to walk off the pain.

****

Gate 5

The whole crew is a bit drained from the events thus far. They are halfway through the trip, and the mood is somber. Bobby and Lilith, however, continue their vigorous routine of recording the area, and Bobby continues to commentate enthusiastically for his audience. Those two still appear to be jubilant and have not taken on the mood of the other four. As they enter the fifth gate, bobby ups the ante.

"This is the fifth gate," Bobby proclaims. "Legend has it that this is the gate where they say if you call to spirits, they will let themselves be seen."

"What do you mean, we just call out to them?" Jose asks.

"No," Bobby answers. "We need to call them out with a ritual, a séance."

"Okay," Roger responds. "Let's do it."

"Wait a minute," Clyde says with trepidation. "We are just gonna evoke evil spirits? What good can come out of that?"

"Come on, man," Roger retorts. "You're the toughest guy here. What's the worst that could happen?"

"Yeah, evoking spirits," Jose responds somewhat reluctantly.

"I'm up for it," Demi agrees.

"We all need to hold hands," Bobby explains.

"But we are evoking spirits that we might not want to encounter?" Clyde asks.

"Stop being a bitch!" Roger shouts.

"Do you think by walking through the seven gates of hell you are somehow redeeming your soul?" A few seconds of silence follow. "Let's get the full experience," Roger states. "We've come this far, and we are lucky enough to have Bobby here with us. And let's not forget, we are on camera. Do you want people all over the country calling you a pussy?"

"I'm good," Clyde says adamantly. "And I want that last part cut out of the video, or I'm suing you guys." Clyde looks into the camera. "I'm the fucking séance master, bro! I ain't scared of shit!" he shouts toughly. "You can keep that take," Clyde says softly.

Everyone locks hands, except Lilith, who holds the camera steady on the group. As they lock hands, Bobby takes control. He lights up eight candles and puts them in a circle just before gate five. All five of them stand inside the circle, except for Lilith, who continues filming from different angles.

"We are here to walk the seven gates of hell. We are at gate number five. Are there any spirit here that want to say something? You can knock on something or make a noise. We are all going to be quiet and listen." The group continues to hold hands. Everyone stays silent and listens for a response from any spirits occupying the area. After a few minutes of complete silence, Bobby continues, "Is anyone here?" They all open their eyes and look at each other. No sounds are heard. They let go of each other's hands. Just as they do, they hear a faint voice say, "*Turn back now*."

"Did you guys hear that?" Roger shouts.

"I heard someone say, 'turn back now!'" Demi says.

"So did I," Clyde responds.

"Me too," says Jose. The voice sounds almost like a record playing backward on a turntable.

"Lock hands again," Bobby commands. They all do so. "Do you want to tell us something?" Bobby asks. A few seconds of silence go by.

"*Turn around now!*" a strange-sounding voice utters in stereo.

"Who said that?" Roger shouts.

"Wasn't me!" Clyde blurts out.

"Did you guys hear that?" Roger asks.

"Yes," they all respond.

"Someone is throwing their voice, clearly," Clyde shouts.

"I think it's the camera lady!" Jose proclaims. Lilith moves the camera away from her face and looks at Jose with contempt, and scoffs.

"That was definitely someone from beyond," Bobby asserts.

"Try it again," Demi says. "This is awesome!"

"What happens if we don't turn around?" Bobby asks.

"*Death to all!*" the strange-sounding voice says.

"What the fuck?" Clyde asks.

"I heard 'death to all,'" Jose says.

"Okay, cute trick, Bobby," Rogers alleges. "Let's get moving."

"I'm not seeing how he could have done that?" Demi says.

"He probably has someone up on the train tracks playing a recording," Roger says.

"Yeah, that makes sense," Jose states.

"I'm not responsible for those

voices," Bobby claims.

"Dude, good trick, though!" Clyde responds. "You almost had me! Really enhances the experience." They all walk through gate number five, the widest gate and the first to have two car lanes.

****

Gate 6

The sixth gate is only a nine-minute walk from gate five. Gate six has the most bushes and trees surrounding it. The train tracks haven't been used in many years, and the grass is very high on each side of the dirt road leading to the gate. Bushes and grass have even reclaimed the tracks above. This is the most dilapidated and creepiest looking gate thus far.

"It is said that if you stand in gate six at night, you will be able to hear a car coming, that never comes," Bobby mentions. "Legend has it that *Carl* and *Adam Boyd*, bothers, rode their car through all seven gates and are still trying to find their way back to the land of the living. So, they drive through gate six every night and then disappear or something like that. They call it the *'ghost car gate.'*"

"Well, then, let's try it out!" Roger responds and then hustles over to the gate and stands inside. The others casually walk over while waiting for Roger to report his findings.

"Anything?" Demi asks.

"Not yet," Roger yells out. The rest of the crew reaches the gate, and all stand underneath.

"This gate is creepy as hell, no pun intended," Clyde offers.

"What's that sound?" Jose says.

"What sound?" Roger responds skeptically.

"Wait, I hear something!" Demi says.

"Oh, shit, it's a car! We gotta get out of here; we'll be killed!" Clyde says anxiously. "I ain't getting fucking hit again!"

"Wait!" Bobby shouts, just as the group begins to disperse. He grabs Clyde's arm. "It's the ghost car!"

"How the fuck you know that?" Roger asks.

"Cause there are no cars on this road.

This road has been closed for years!" Bobby replies.

"Maybe some idiot doesn't know that or doesn't care," Jose responds.

"No, no," Bobby says, "it's virtually impossible to get a car on this road. They closed off the entrance and exit several years ago!"

"And yet, there is a car approaching fast!" Clyde says facetiously. "It's getting louder! I'm not getting hit by another God damned care, man!"

"Just hold your positions, trust me!" Bobby shouts. The gate is small and can barely fit one car through it. All of them hold tight. Clyde, Jose, and Roger cringe. The approaching car sound gets louder and louder until it feels like it is seconds from being upon them. Suddenly, they see headlights coming around the turn. A few seconds, at best, separate them from the approaching vehicle. No one had time to move. They were like deer in headlights. They all scream and brace for impact. The car is moving so fast that they don't have time to react any other way.

Zoom!

The car runs directly through them and continues past them. They had all closed their eyes and braced for impact, except for Jose. However, the car seemingly went right through them.

"What the fuck was that?" Roger screams.

"I believe that was the 'ghost car,'" Bobby says.

"That car went right through us!" Demi says in amazement.

"That was some *Twilight Zone* shit, bro!" Clyde mentions.

"I saw the mother fuckers!" Jose shouts.

"Saw who?" Roger asks.

"The driver and the passenger," Jose responds. "You all had your eyes closed. I was looking right at them. I looked directly into the driver's eyes. He was terrified. Not because of us. He was just terrified in general."

"You saw him?" Clyde asks.

"Yeah," Jose responds. "He looked right at me, but I don't think he saw us. He was more scared than me!"

"What did he look like?"

"I don't know," Jose says, "some white dude with brown hair. You guys all look alike and shit."

"That was some crazy shit, guys!" Roger exclaims.

"Are we sure a damn car just came through the tunnel and ran us over, yet, we didn't get hit?" Clyde says. "I'm beginning to think we are all losing it, man!"

"Carl Boyd was a white man with brown hair, legend has it," Bobby mentions.

"Yo, that's crazy!" Jose says.

"We have a fifteen-minute walk to gate number seven, and we have to be there by midnight," Bobby warns. "We'd better get moving if we want to make it in time for midnight."

****

Gate 7

Twenty minutes later, the group reaches gate seven. After the long journey, they are all relieved to almost be done. Still, they are anxious and eager to find out what will happen when they cross gate seven at midnight.

"It's 11:52," Demi says. "We have seven minutes."

"I have the same time," Bobby mentions.

"I don't know about this?" Jose says. "We've seen some freaky shit. I think this might be a mistake."

"You're the one who brought us here, dumbass!" Roger states. "Now you wanna bail like a little girl?"

"I don't think it's being a little girl after getting run over by a car that never touched us," Jose responds.

"I swear if you try to bail now, I will personally throw you through this gate myself!" Roger says resolutely.

"Jose, you ever hear of the three men who were told that today was their last day on earth and asked how they will spend it?" Bobby asks.

"No, is this some stupid riddle?" Jose replies.

"Kind of," Bobby responds. Jose shrugs his shoulder.

"Okay," he responds. Bobby proceeds.

"The first man says, 'I'm gonna drink as much alcohol as I can.' The second said, 'I'm gonna get three hookers and have as much sex as possible.' The third said, 'I shall finish the game!' I shall finish the game."

"Okay, Young Guns," Roger gests sarcastically. "You're Emilio Estevez now?"

"That was some deep shit, though," Clyde states.

"I think the answers would be a bit different if they asked three women," Demi states. "The first would say, 'I'm gonna go shopping until I run out of money.' The second would say, 'I'm gonna call all my friends and family and tell them I love them.' And the third would say, 'Are you sure I only have one more day? Where did you get this information? Can I speak to your manager?' Women are just smarter than men, I guess!" Everyone starts laughing.

"Can I speak to your manager," Clyde repeats as he starts cracking up. "Okay, Karen!"

"Twenty seconds till midnight!" Bobby announces. They all wait anxiously. Roger leads the countdown starting with ten seconds remaining. The rest join in like it's New Year's Eve. When they hit zero, they all walk through gate number seven.

They cross through the gate and stop and wait a few seconds.

"See, nothing happened!" Roger exclaims. "I told you all this is bullshit!"

"Where did Bobby and Lilith go?" Demi asks the others.

"They were right behind us," Clyde replies.

"Maybe they were too scared to come through!" Jose states.

"Yeah," Clyde says, "he was acting all cool, but I felt like he was a big pussy."

"But where is he?" Demi asks. She looks back toward gate seven with her flashlight and sees nothing.

"They probably moved to the side and dipped as soon as we walked through," Roger postulates. Demi looks confused as she continues to inspect the area where they came through. "Guys!" Demi says just above a whisper. She is still transfixed on the gate seven entrance.

"So, that means we gotta walk all the way back to our car," Jose says.

"Guys!" Demi says a little louder this time.

"Yeah," Clyde responds. "That asshole said he had a friend meeting him here that would give us a ride back to our car."

"Guys!" Demi screams. "Where the fuck is gate seven?"

"Huh," Roger says. He turns around. Clyde and Jose turn around a second later. They look back and see only woods. There is no gate seven.

"What the..." Jose says in shock.

"The mother fucker disappeared!" Clyde yells anxiously.

"Wait a minute," Roger says calmly, "wasn't the gate right here? We only took a few steps in at best."

"The gate was right here, man!" Clyde screams. "What the hell is going on?"

Seconds later, the sound of dogs barking and growling can be heard in the distance.

"What the hell was that?" Demi asks the group.

"Probably nothing," Roger responds. "Just some dogs barking and growling in the distance," Jose replies. "I hear that all the time in my hood."

The barking sounds get louder and louder, however. So much so that they appear to be quickly approaching.

"Ah, maybe we should get out of here?" Clyde suggests.

"Yeah, those wild dogs are getting close," Jose says. Within seconds, however, the group shines their flashlights into the forest area ahead and notice several glowing eyes glaring through the trees ahead staring at them.

"What the fuck is that, bro?" Clyde says in angst.

"I don't know," Roger replies.

Bobby and Lilith suddenly step out into the open from behind a big tree and bushes where the glowing eyes are located. They are dressed very differently. Bobby is wearing a red suit with a black shirt with two large red horns sticking out of the front of his head. Lilith is wearing a long black dress with black horns sticking out of the sides of her head.

"Congratulations!" Bobby says in a creepy, distorted voice. "You finally made it to your final destination!" Both Bobby and Lilith start laughing.

Just then, ten hounds of hell come forward and make themselves seen. They are not like any dogs that anyone has ever seen on this earth. They are larger and more ferocious looking than any dogs any human has ever witnessed. They look more like four-legged werewolves. Their ribs are exposed, and they look more like zombie dogs.

"Run!" Demi shouts!

They all run in different directions. The ferocious hounds give chase! Two of them jump on Demi's back, sending her to the ground.

Crunch!!!

The sound of teeth biting through flesh and bone echo into the night, along with screams of agony and terror!

****

Two Days Later

A man walks into a local dive bar on the outskirts of *Willville*. Country music is playing loudly on the jukebox. His head is down. He walks through the door as two other men are walking out. His shoulder inadvertently crashes into one of the men. He keeps walking, unphased by the encounter. Both men stop, turn and look at him. The man whose shoulder he collided with shouts, "Hey, what's your problem, man?" as he changes course and heads toward the rude stranger for a confrontation. His buddy grabs his arm and whispers something to him. "Oh," the offended man says, then abruptly turns and walks out the door.

It's late, and there are only a few people left. The man walks up and sits at the bar. No one is near him.

"Hey, *Jack*," the female bartender says consolingly. "What are ya having?"

"Whatever you drink when your daughter is missing, and you want the pain to go away," Jack says in a somber tone.

"They haven't found her yet?" She asks. Jack looks down at the shot that the bartender just poured him and shakes his head side to side slowly and methodically. He grabs the shot and jolts it quickly into his mouth. As his head leans back, he notices the T.V. above. *'Breaking News,'* in big, bold letters. Underneath the subtitle, *'The Four Missing Person Found at 7 Gates.'*

"Turn it up, *Jenny!*" Jack yells and mumbles at the same time.

"Huh?" Jenny asks, confused.

"The T.V.! the T.V!" Jacks shouts clearly this time, pointing up at it. "Turn it up now!" Jenny turns and sees the headline on the screen, and her demeanor changes immediately. She rushes anxiously for the remote. The faces of the missing four pop up on the screen. She turns the volume up and mutes the jukebox as fast as she can.

"Hey, I like that song!" some drunk objects from the pool table.

"Shut up, *Earl!*" both Jack and Jenny scream in unison. Earl cowers, raising his hands up, and accidentally drops his pool stick in the process.

The faces fade as a reporter comes on the T.V. and says, "The police have released the footage of what happened to those four missing persons at what legend calls, *'The Seven Gates of Hell.'* We warn you; this footage is very disturbing. Please watch at your own risk!"

Roger, Clyde, Jose, and Demi are all lined up at the edge of a cliff that is just past gate number seven. Lilith is filming from a distance where she has all four of them in her camera lens from behind but on an angle. And all four are stiffly facing straight ahead over the edge, toward the abyss. The depth of the drop cannot be determined on the camera, but the locals know it to be steep enough and far enough to kill anyone who dares to jump.

"What are you guys doing?" Bobby screams, just off-camera. Roger looks back at the camera. His body remains still, facing the edge. His face, expressionless.

"We came here tonight not to find hell, but to find peace," Roger explains calmly, robotically. Roger turns back toward the edge, and Demi turns toward the camera with the same robotic, emotionless stare.

"We believe that the real hell is this life!" Demi proclaims. Jack's eyes well up with tears. Demi turns back, and Clyde turns his head toward the camera.

"We will find in death what we could

not find in this life," Clyde also says calmly and robotically, like the other two before him. He turns his head back toward the edge. Jose then turns his head toward the camera and stares at it for a second with a menacing look.

"Acceptance!" Jose says confidently and very creepily. He turns his head back toward the edge. The group then locks hands. Roger's right-hand locks with Demi's left; Demi's right-hand locks with Clyde's left; and Clyde's right-hand locks with Jose's left.

"Don't do this, you guys, please!" Bobby screams as he steps into view of the camera.

Without hesitation, the four take one step forward in unison and drop swiftly off the edge of the cliff. Not one of them makes a sound as they fall to their deaths.

"Oh, no!" Bobby cries in awe. "What just happened," he yells, looking at the camera as if he is looking at Lilith.

Lilith remains steady. Her view is through the camera's eye only. She walks over to the edge of the mountain with the camera on her right shoulder. The audience at home stares through her lens. She reaches the edge, where the four had just taken their last steps. She angles the camera down, anticipating where the group might have landed. The bodies of the group of four are lying far below the cliff, mangled and disfigured. She focuses in as the news footage fades out...

The End

Make sure that you check out Will's horror trilogy… "*The Whistling Man* & *The Whitling Man 2*," on sale NOW!

Also, the terrifying, "*Nomed Station*."

Please visit:

https://willsavive.com/

Facebook Fan Page (A must for all horror fans – get all the latest news on all things horror related):

https://www.facebook.com/dawhistlingman